THE DEPARTMENT FOR

MUTATED PERSONS

ROBERT R. FIKE

Copyright © 2019 by Robert R. Fike

Robert R. Fike
1402 W Rosewood Ave
San Antonio, TX 78201

Printed in the United States of America.

First Edition

To my wife, Damaris, for humoring my chaotic brain as it bounced between characters, dialogue, and storylines. Thank you for being a fan and listening when it felt like everyone was silent. Thank you for the mother, wife, and woman you are.

To all the people who helped by reading and critiquing this work: THANK YOU. Thank you to Rhonda, Juliette, Jon, Sherri, and several members of Wattpad for investing their time and passion.

Thank you to my parents, who let a kid spend long road trips with headphones in and a pen scrawling across a notebook.

This story is for anyone who has ever felt less than.

You are mighty.

one

It was another summer day in Arizona: arid, sun-soaked, eternal. Alan never owned a pair of sunglasses. Nineteen years spent squinting. Something in his heart said sunny days were behind him.

The block was government zoned; police enforcement at every corner and no civilians in sight except for Alan. Wide two-lane streets: empty. Not a scrap of garbage. Clean, deserted, and sterile.

Alan stood across the street from the white government building, and adjusted the bag slung over his slouched left shoulder. He brandished an emotionless, straight smile. His amber eyes stared up at the light-blotting structure, shadow reaching out toward him as if emboldened by the police presence.

Alan ran a hand through his short brown hair, then pulled his hand back to the sling of his pack to brace it from falling onto the pavement. Alan found a loose piece of sidewalk rock and scraped a long white line across the ground like rough chalk writing. He was fussing with this red hoodie when a voice snapped the air like a twig.

"Hey! Get over here."

Alan looked to his left and saw a large man in black military gear staring back intensely. Alan assumed he was staring. The man's eyes were covered with sunglasses, and a taut, fabric mask was covering his mouth. The lack of visible facial features gave way to anxious assumptions for Alan; namely, the man's stiff posture and a hand near his firearm. The man looked down at Alan's long chalk mark and then back up at Alan.

"Do you have papers?" The man asked sharply, a condescending finger pointing at Alan. His voice was deep, strong, and impatient, so Alan didn't feel like talking back like he normally would.

Alan reached backward and pulled his bag off his shoulders. He balanced it uneasily on his hip, then nervously pulled a crinkled red slip of paper from its zippered pouch. The man snatched the paper from Alan's hand with little regard for Alan's personal space. The man's head bent down to acknowledge he was reading Alan's credentials.

"I'm sorry, I didn't know I couldn't...," Alan attempted to answer, his voice awkward and his words fumbling. He could feel the temperature on his skin rising and the hairs on his arms tingling. His joints suddenly ached and the hairs on his neck were trying to pry themselves free from his body.

With little more than a groaning response to Alan's explanation, the man shoved a muscular arm outstretched with the paper. Alan took the paper back, a tattered mess of red, wrinkled paper. The man thrust his arm out, pointing a gloved index finger across the street at the white building, which stared down at them both with dispassionate dominance; its mere existence was meant to define their realities.

The operative reached down and picked up an errant scrap of paper from the sidewalk and shoved it into his body armor jacket before Alan could ask for it back. Alan looked down at his crinkled dossier paper, then back up at the man in black. The operative cleared his throat angrily.

"Move along, freak."

Alan's face tensed at the word. Freak? The word made his stomach turn. The tingling wasn't going away. Was it permanent now? Had Alan's brain broken under the man's cold visage?

"Did you hear me? Move. Along."

Alan nodded nervously and set a foot onto the asphalt to show the officer he was en route. The man turned away and began walking back down the sidewalk toward another police officer, who had been keeping an eye on the situation from a small white car. Alan watched as the man who had accosted him shook his head at the other officer and waved his arm back in Alan's direction. The other officer shook his head as well, pulled an arm up to the square walkie-talkie attached to his shoulder and muttered something into the microphone. He unclicked the comm button and gave Alan a passing glance through sunglasses; then he looked at the building across the way.

Alan took the hint and managed a few quick steps all the way across the street and up to the white government office building that stuck out against the rest of the city landscape.

The words were etched perfectly into the stone face: The United States Department for Mutated Persons, Precinct 305. Not a scrap of trash around the entrance. Nobody for miles, aside from law enforcement. Alan mused that this was a small reminder of the times they were living in. It was a distinct contrast from what his parents used to talk about, the stories they painted, and the people they once were. But that was then, and this was now.

Alan pushed his way through the revolving doorway of the 305 building and was met with a cold room with a high ceiling, granite floor tiles, and marble columns. At the end of the long room stood a granite lobby desk, a woman seated behind it, typing and answering the entryway phone. She did not look up when he entered, nor did she give any indication that she had even remotely recognized his presence in the empty room.

Alan cleared his throat. The woman looked up, her eyes both annoyed and bored. She glanced back down at her computer screen, without regard for Alan's presence. Alan walked up to the desk and slipped his bag onto the floor.

"Please do not leave your things on the floor," the woman said in a terse manner, letting out a sigh of discontent afterward. Alan reluctantly pulled the bag back up over his shoulder. "Papers."

Alan held out his red slip of paper - a wrinkled, fading mess - and the woman took it without looking at him again.

"I wasn't sure if I should call ahead, but obviously you've got a lot of people today," Alan joked hesitantly, looking around at the empty room.

The woman didn't look up. Instead, she ran a black pen across the red paper in a rote, measured movement she'd likely done thousands of times before. Name. Region. Job Code. Blah, blah, blah. She rolled her eyes, and raised the red paper back up into Alan's face.

"Take this in, and Secretary Hollins will be with you shortly, Mr. Mitchell."

Alan nodded silently; the woman never made eye contact again and thus did not acknowledge his nonverbal. She cleared her throat and spoke sternly, "Move along."

The woman's desk phone rang again - one ring - and she picked it up right away. Alan walked past her to the frosted door behind the desk and entered into the office of Secretary Roger Hollins. Hollins was standing behind a giant oak desk, a tiny American flag nestled inside a coffee cup on top. Alan could swear he smelled the wood still. Everything was rust, bronze and brown, which made the flag - with its fading red, white and blue - stick out. Alan wondered what the flag meant to Hollins; he wondered what it meant to anyone anymore. The patriotic tones were fading on the flag, just like they had in Alan's mind.

"Let's see the paper, son," Hollins said with his back to Alan and his hand out in anticipation. His voice was paternal and lethargic, an almost disarming quality if it weren't for the circumstances of their meeting.

Alan handed over the red slip, and Hollins turned to greet the paper, but not Alan. Hollins, a tall blocky man with gray hair and a large, blunt nose, stared at Alan's red paper through cheater eyeglasses.

Alan attempted to sit down in the rust-red, leather chair across from Hollins's desk. Hollins sucked in a quick, loud breath, his eyes looking up at Alan briefly.

"That won't be necessary," Hollins said.

Alan stood back up awkwardly, his bag falling down into the seat beneath him. Hollins cleared his throat, his eyes staring intently at the red slip.

"Don't scuff the leather, son," Hollins reprimanded Alan like an annoyed father. It reminded Alan a little bit of his old cross-country coach, who always seemed annoyed by the athletes leaving their bags on the locker room benches.

Alan pulled the backpack up to his shoulder again, the skin feeling raw beneath his worn cotton hooded sweatshirt. Hollins groaned, his lips pursing and parting as he read the slip to himself. He noticed the cherry red, metallic stapler on his desk rattling softly on the wood surface, taking on an air of nervousness. Hollins looked up from the paper at the skinny boy, no older than nineteen years, staring awkwardly at the floor.

"Magnetism, huh? Don't meet a lot of metal movers around here. Please try to keep your hands and mind to yourself, son. That's government property."

Alan looked up, and the stapler stopped vibrating. Hollins cleared his throat, a strange habit meant to transition to a new subject.

"Alright, then," Hollins sighed and pressed the intercom button on his desk phone, "Miss Doland, please call transportation. We'll be sending Mr. Mitchell to the 308."

"Yes, sir."

The phone hung up, and Hollins pulled his finger back. He took out a black pen from his coffee cup, shaking the flag out of the cup and onto his desk in the process. Alan stared down at the flag, the cheap cloth rolled over the stick like a snake strangling its prey. Hollins made a few marks on the paper, and then signed the bottom half.

"You will exit this building, give this paper to the driver outside, and find your quarters at the 308 station house. They will be expecting you in one hour, so don't think you can lag behind on this. Dismissed."

Hollins handed Alan the red paper, and then pointed to the door in a strange, detached mood. Alan walked out into the empty room, where Miss Doland - still the same apathetic girl - was still busily talking on the phone while simultaneously scanning a large phone book. A quick glance at the paper only confirmed that there were lists of numbers, presumably codes that Alan would never understand nor never care to. He looked down at his red paper:

Confirmed mutation. Designated for work. 308.

Hollins's signature was scrawled in the bottom right corner, a sloppy cursive that Alan only guessed was his name. Alan wondered why people wrote their names in such a haphazard, rushed manner. He long mused it was from the busyness of everyday work, but Hollins wasn't busy; just rushed. Now Alan gathered that it had little to do with Hollins's view of his own time, but more to do with how little he valued Alan's time or presence in his midst. Alan cleared his throat to get Miss Doland's attention.

"Please wait outside," Miss Doland said in a cold, threatening manner, her arm outstretched and pointing toward the exit.

Alan put his head down and walked outside, where a white transit van was now waiting for him. The streets were still empty aside from the van, and the law enforcement agents walking back and forth in precise formation. Alan opened the back passenger door and stepped into the pristine van.

"Alan Mitchell?" a screen lit up, a digital flutter in its voice. The computer prompt popped up on the panel that would've been the driver's headrest. The van was empty, a self-driving model implemented by the government to transport the mutated. The prompt displayed Alan's full name, a question mark, with a yes or no option below. Alan pressed his finger to the glass.

"Thank you. Setting destination: work precinct, designation 308. Please buckle your seatbelt."

Alan lifted his hand and watched as the metal seat buckle floated up in the air around his lap. Using his powers in a non-government sanctioned fashion felt like one last act of defiance. The buckle rolled over itself, resisting Alan's palm as he moved it back and forth in midair.

"Please fasten your seatbelt now."

The voice was monotone, but to Alan it felt authoritative and angry. Alan snapped out of his trance and put the belt down with his hands. He shoved his bag off to the other seat and watched the windows around himself tint. People on the streets wouldn't even know it was him. They wouldn't know where he was going, what he was doing. He was redacted. Soon, his own parents would cease to remember the little boy who had broken the backyard slide by popping all of the screws out at once. That boy was gone anyway. Now, the man would be gone too. And nobody cared.

two

"Welcome to Work Precinct 308," the robotic voice chimed from the self-driving car's white dashboard. Alan opened his eyes after a restless sleep, his mind fumbling through a groggy stupor as his brain tried to right itself.

Alan couldn't be certain how long the trip had taken or how long he had slept, but neither seemed to align with each other. The fogginess still floated in his brain. Sleep would do that. Nothing could be for certain.

The car stopped gently, and the windows slowly transitioned from opaque to transparent, revealing Alan's new home for the foreseeable future. It was an old apartment complex, mostly concrete with soft edges, with blacked out windows and strong metal doors with bars and a large wall all the way around. The front office was designed like a hotel with an awning resting just over the car Alan was in. The entire sight was bathed in the slowly setting afternoon sun.

"Please exit the vehicle," the voice buzzed. The 'please' did not feel as cordial to Alan as perhaps the programmer had envisioned (or maybe it was). It was a facade of decorum, a false sense of politeness that hid cold, detached systemized cattle herding. Alan almost moo'd out of amusement but thought better of it. After all, the machine might be recording his audio. Also, his throat felt a little hoarse from the terrible nap.

The door opened on its own. Alan grabbed his bag and stepped out into the dry, afternoon air. The front office of the complex was the only thing not surrounded by the concrete wall. From what Alan could tell, it was the only entrance and exit for the entire campus.

It was so unbearably hot that Alan took off his red hoodie and shoved it into his backpack. Something in his periphery caught his attention, and Alan looked up from his pack at the front lobby. The front desk's windows were tinted, but Alan could make out a stocky figure coming toward the front door.

The door swung open, and the short, stocky man came out with a clipboard. He looked down at his brown clipboard, his bush mustache wagging back and forth. He ran a hand through his thinning hair, his eyes deeply entranced by his clipboard.

"Alan Mitchell?"

"That's what they call me," Alan joked. The man looked up from his clipboard with a look of busy annoyance. He made a check mark on the paper, and pointed at Alan's bag.

"Bring your things," the man said gruffly, and then stomped back to the front office lobby, shoving the heavy doors wide open to swing back violently on his way in.

The room was unadorned, save for a lone plant in the entryway corner. The white tiled floor was scuffed, and the grout was filled with dirt in aging cracks. A small desk was at the back wall, a stack of papers sloppily hanging off the edge facing Alan. The papers were a mixture of white forms and red slips jammed together unevenly.

"My name is Randall Finch. People around here just call me Finch. I don't care what you call me, just follow the rules. Don't leave the building without telling me, and you'll be fine. Don't invite people to the building, and you'll be fine. Don't tell people on the outside where you live, and you'll be fine. Don't bring liquor or drugs into the building, and you'll be fine. Don't leave your room after lights out, and you'll be fine. Give me your red slip...

14

"... Or spend a night in the box?" Alan interjected, a tiny smirk on his face.

Finch rolled his eyes, and Alan replaced his smirk with a bunched lip awkwardly clinging to the right side of his mouth. Finch released a low, rumbling sigh and held out his right hand.

"Let's get this over with."

Alan stretched his hand out with his paper and Finch tore it out of his hands. Finch looked over the red paper, made some notes then began filling out the paperwork on his clipboard with the red slip guiding him. His pen marks were hard and swift, much like the rest of his actions. He didn't have time for the new guy's jokes. Jokes got people in trouble. Then they got shipped out to the processing center and had to deal with the board of directors. Finch didn't like the questions those visits brought. It complicated things already complicated enough.

Alan noticed beyond the desk there was a door that led out into the courtyard of the complex. There were people hanging out in the green patch of land; the only green patch Alan could remember seeing in his journey to his new home. A few palm trees surrounded a circular grass area with an empty swimming pool. But Alan didn't realize he was staring at a group of guys who were sitting in plastic lawn chairs in the courtyard, but they had noticed. The men looked at each other and got up from their seats, pushing their way into the lobby.

"Hey, baby bird, who's the new guy?" the leader of the group - a muscular man with rough facial hair and piercing dark eyes - asked Finch in a unsettling polite tone.

"Baby bird?" Alan asked quietly, setting a sideways glance at Finch. Finch shook his head.

"Shut up, new guy. I'm talking to baby bird," the leader shot back. He rubbed his patchy facial hair and looked back at Finch.

Finch clenched his teeth and pointed at his clipboard, "I don't have time for this crap, Castor. I need to input him in the system so I can clock out. Why don't you take your little entourage back to the courtyard so I can do my damn job."

Castor didn't like that. He grabbed Finch by the arm, Castor's hand turning red hot. Finch winced, his arm heating up and blistering. He let out a pained exhale.

"Don't you ever tell me what to do," Castor said angrily. Finch struggled, but Castor wrenched Finch's arm back and tightened

16

his burning grip. "You normies just think you're better than us. I don't like the way you look down on me."

"Castor, let him go."

Castor looked back at the courtyard doorway where a tall, muscular man was standing. Alan released his fist, and Finch's desk gently came back down onto the floor without everyone noticing. Everyone, except for Marshall, the man in the doorway. He was subtly looking at the desk, when Castor finally let Finch go. Alan looked at Finch's arm, red finger marks burned into his flesh. Finch picked up his clipboard off the ground and started making notes.

"That's another strike for you, Castor. One more, and you'll have to be processed."

"Don't threaten me, baby bird," Castor sneered, and he nodded to his guys. "I'll catch you later, newbie."

Marshall watched, unmoving, as Castor and his friends went back out into the courtyard. Once they were outside, Marshall relaxed his posture and turned his attention to Alan, who was anxiously standing in the middle of the room.

"You'll have to forgive Castor, kid. He wasn't blessed with an abundance of intelligence. You okay, Finch?"

Finch nodded, exhaling a breath of relief. "I'm fine. But Castor? Castor's on his last warning. And we know what comes after that."

"Let me worry about Castor," Marshall said, his eyes staring back at the courtyard. "So, who's the new kid?"

"Alan Mitchell. Just got shipped here from…" Finch looked down at his paperwork, his mind wandering.

"The 305 I guess," Alan replied, his tone carrying a pinch of detached confusion. It was just a bunch of numbers to him. He wasn't from St. Louis, Phoenix, San Antonio, Chicago. He was a punched up zip code kid. It was best to forget he had ever lived anywhere else at all. Finch looked up from his clipboard, unamused by Alan's interjection into the conversation.

"Yeah… the 305," Finch said, his displeasure seeping out slowly with his drawn out words. He looked over to Marshall, who was standing with arms crossed next to them. "I'm going to file this paperwork. Alan's in room 224b. Can you show him around, Marshall?"

Marshall looked at Alan, sizing him up with a discerning eye. "Sure thing, Finch. Come on, kid. Let's see if we can get you into some trouble."

"No trouble," Finch chided as Marshall and Mitchell walked through to the courtyard, where Castor was still sulking. Marshall put a hand on Alan's shoulder and pointed around the area. It was more a sign to Castor that Marshall was looking out for the kid than a genuine act of friendship, but Alan appreciated it anyway.

"The cafeteria is down at the end of the courtyard here. Mostly just the old high school stuff. Pizza day on Friday, so that doesn't completely suck. We go grocery shopping in groups on Wednesday, so you'll want to use your credits to get snacks then. They'll bring you soap and toothpaste and that kind of stuff, so don't waste your credits on it in the store. Your room is on the second floor."

Marshall ushered Alan up a metal staircase blasted with white paint, chips of it flaking in well-trafficked areas. They finally got to his room, and Marshall showed him in. The room was a single bed, wrapped in white sheets with brown carpeting on the floor and a small bathroom. It was about as dingy a hotel room as Alan could remember seeing before. He looked back at the front door.

"No lock?" Alan asked.

"Nope. Nobody has locks. It seems kinda pointless since we're not allowed to leave and there's cameras all over the place. If someone steals your stuff just let me know. We tend to take care of matters on our own. Keeps the board out of it."

"I heard Finch mention them earlier. They don't sound great."

Marshall stopped for a moment, looking out the curtain-draped window of the room. Castor's friends had left and they had been replaced with a group talking down at the empty swimming pool, their legs dangling over the edge. Marshall seemed to be thinking about something far off.

"No. They aren't 'great.' If you see the board, then you're screwed. So don't get yourself into trouble. Anything else?"

Marshall asked the question more for himself, his eyes pensively looking to the popcorn ceiling trying to muster another thought. He snapped his fingers and pointed at Alan, a big grin on his face.

"Marshall and Mitchell. I just realized that. That's us, kid. Anyway, that was the whole show. You need anything from me?"

Alan shook his head, so Marshall went for the exit.

"Wait. What do we do here?" Alan asked. No one had ever told him. Since he received his red slip, no one had told him what exactly he was in for. Marshall turned around, his lips curled down and his eyes blinking slowly.

"It's a work camp, kid. We do what they tell us to do."

Marshall's voice was deflated, realizing Alan didn't know what he was in for and sad for all the people working in the 308. It was a work camp; there wasn't anything more to it than that. Alan didn't respond, so Marshall broke the awkward silence.

"Dinner's at 6. Don't be late. If you can believe it, the food gets worse."

three

"Get up, Mr. Mitchell!" Finch's voice rang like a morning bell inside Alan's brain.

Alan felt Finch's gravelly tone bounce between Alan's ears with thunderous resound, shaking his weak bones to life. Alan hardly slept at all his first night in the 308, and now Finch was shouting for him to meet the new day.

"It's still dark out," Alan said with one half-open eye, his voice scratchy and strained.

Alan pulled his upper body up out of bed, leaning on the bed with his forearms. The courtyard was still dark, with fluorescents providing sickly, white light. Alan looked up at Finch, whose mustache was bunched up to one side, his eyes narrowing at each passing second. Finch cocked his head to the side, then shook it.

"Bus comes in twenty minutes, and you're going to be on it," Finch said gruffly and then he pulled his bottom teeth against his mustache while he adjusted the brown leather belt in his beige pant loops.

Alan rubbed his eyes and looked around at his new home. Cracked drywall. Patchy carpet. Dripping sink faucet. Alan scrambled his hair and got up out of bed. He pulled his sheets back over his lumpy mattress. Then he bent backwards and felt his back audibly pop. He groaned and walked over to his dresser.

"That's the spirit. We're meeting down in the lobby when you're dressed," Finch responded, his voice trailing off as his mind began moving on to the next worker on his checklist.

"What should I wear?" Alan asked, looking into his sparsely packed dresser.

Finch - broken up from his workflow - exhaled an exasperated breath and checked Alan's name off his clipboard list with one violent pen stroke. He pointed with his thumb at the open doorway.

"Just wear what you got, kid. We'll have uniforms on-site."

The lobby was filled with the rest of the occupants of the complex. There were plenty of new faces that Alan couldn't place. He recognized a few people from the swimming pool, and Castor - his unkempt facial hair hiding thin, frowning lips – rolled his eyes when the two made eye contact at the front entrance.

23

Alan finally saw Marshall, who was socializing with a group of people around Finch's desk. Marshall gave Alan a big grin and waved him over to their group.

"Hey Alan, meet the guys," Marshall shouted, his mouth stretched with a humongous smile. Alan closed the distance between them and looked around at this new group of neighbors.

"Guys?" a girl in the group chided, her head cocked to the side as she stared Marshall down with a raised eyebrow and sideways grin.

Marshall acknowledged her, his hands raised to the air,d "People? Persons? Humans? You get what I'm saying, Athena."

Athena smirked back at Marshall, a bounce in her shoulders from a silent laugh. Her brown eyes were soft and they jokingly rolled at Marshall's backpedaling. Marshall shrugged his shoulders and laughed in a jovial tone. Thank goodness for a group who appreciated a little humor. Maybe he could fit in that way.

"...or freaks? The government stooges seem to like that one," Alan joked, his voice trailing off as he saw everyone's face shrink from smile to disgust at the sight of him.

The group was silent. Their faces were long with flattened lips, and sunken eyes. One of the men, a gray-haired man named George, looked at Marshall with raised eyebrows and an insistent

24

nod. The group slowly started taking steps toward the lobby entrance, and Marshall hung back. He gave Alan a pat on the back and leaned down to Alan's eye level.

"Yeah, maybe not bring that one up next time, kid," Marshall said under his breath, and then addressed the group that was walking away, "Anyway, you guys ready for another day at the construction site? I hear we're building the frame today."

Most of the gathered friends groaned, while others just nodded weakly. Nevertheless, Marshall continued to smile and bring the rest of them together as their typical morning ritual moved along. He was about to start with another one of his patented Marshall motivational speeches when Finch erupted.

"Alright, bus is here. Everybody out," Finch shouted at the front door. The workers walked out the door. Finch grumbled under his breath, "I Swear the only peace and quiet I get is when you all leave."

The bus was an old commuter transport that had been refitted for the specific task of shipping workers to job sites. The windows were tinted jet black, and the driver seat was taken out in favor of a self-driving computer. The seats were upholstered in old colorful patterns, splashes of color in a gray, concrete world, clearly leftover from whatever their original purpose was.

Alan uncomfortably bounced from row to row, his body not used to the small clearance in the aisle between seats. Alan bumped into one of the workers trying to argue over a window seat. It was Castor. Castor let out a low growl, and a hand grabbed Alan's and pulled him forward down the row.

"Maybe you should give Castor some space," Athena said, and she looked at morose Castor's sunken gaze, "*A lot of* space."

"You're probably right."

The ride was a twenty-minute trek of several city blocks. Alan could see people passing on the sidewalks; people who couldn't see him or anyone else in the bus. They were invisible, migrant workers etching out their day apart from the rest of the world. Not one person on the outside made eye contact with the bus as it traveled to the work site. Not one made notice of the people working to build their streets, office buildings. They all just carried on, blissfully unaware that there was a second set of citizens underneath the veneer.

Alan was woken up from his thoughtful trance by the bus brakes hissing. The vehicle halted in front of a large fenced-off lot with large yellow construction signs and angry red warning letters: *Government Work Zone. Keep Out.*

"Please exit the vehicle," the bus computer chimed, and everybody shambled down the row in a rhythmic left-right-left-right beat.

The chain link gate opened, and several supervisors walked forward, hard hats and glaring faces ready for their rebellious employees. Alan found himself funneled into the construction site, a concrete slab foundation with metal beams, rebar, and a small collection of construction tools strewn about for the day's work.

A food truck - a banged up, off-white, repurposed ice cream truck - was parked off to the side where they would be getting their meals during the work day. Alan noticed Castor, with heaving breaths, push his way through to the food truck. He presumed Castor was famished after a long night of bullying, but then Castor got into the truck.

"Wait, Castor's the cook?" Alan asked, jokingly.

"Government employment at its finest," Marshall replied. The pair chuckled.

"What's wrong with being the cook?" Athena retorted with a smirk, pushing her way out of the work line. Athena began walking toward the truck and turned back as she pedaled backwards toward the truck, "Some of us find serenity in eggs and bacon."

"Won't argue with that," Marshall shouted his reply through a cupped hand at Athena. She rolled her eyes and hopped up into the truck with surly Castor.

Marshall and Alan were carried through the stream of people to the front of the convergence. A couple of supervisors were standing up on the concrete foundation, with a pair of clipboards and a single shared bullhorn.

"Quiet!" a supervisor shouted over the bullhorn, the sound bouncing around the open lot. "Give us your full attention."

The supervisor waited for the clamor to die down, then his partner began again.

"Okay, today we will be placing beams around the foundation. Assignments will be handed out as such: Magnets will move beams. Eyes will weld pieces together. Muscle will be here for safety. If you don't fit in these categories you are a floater, and we will find you something to do.

"Don't idle. Don't cause trouble, and we'll get out to lunch on time. Troublemakers will be docked points. Extreme violators will be given a strike. A member of the board's supervisory unit is on-site for those of you who are already on your second strike. Be careful, keep calm, and we will make this a great workday. Thank you."

The other supervisor began barking names and designations. Most of the crowd seemed to be ignoring him. Dozens of voices broke out into humming chatter as the supervisor continued to belt out names over the din. Alan started to drown in the waves of vocal mixtures.

"A. Mitchell, Magnet!"

Marshall put a hand on Alan's shoulder and pointed him over to a large trailer where the crowd was grabbing equipment. "Come on, A. Mitchell. We've got work to do. Grab your hard hat and orange vest. Safety first," Marshall instructed sarcastically. "This part goes on your head."

Marshall gingerly dropped the hard hat on Alan's head, the orange plastic smothering his eyes.

"You may need to adjust it."

"Gee, thanks for the pointer," Alan replied sardonically, and he shifted the hat on his head so he could see again. Marshall put on his yellow vest, denoting his status as an Eye. These individuals emitted concentrated light out of their eyes; light so powerful that it could melt metals and weld them together if carefully controlled. Another orange vested came over to Alan. His name tag: Nick.

"Hey, Nick."

Nick looked down at his name tag with an unamused frown on his face, "Yeah, ok… We're supposed to move the beams into place. I'll show you where to go. Since you're new, you'll be a support staff for the movers right now. When you get the hang of moving beams, we'll talk about bigger responsibilities."

Alan nodded, and Nick showed him over to their spot. He wasn't really interested in more responsibility. What did he have to look forward to: Head serf? No, he was resigned to do his time. It was what he deserved. But he didn't have to enjoy it, and he certainly didn't have to be invested in the system that was using him for labor.

Nick showed Alan over to a squared off area, lined with dashed yellow markings. A supervisor stood in the center and motioned to the metal beams stacked next to them. Nick gave Alan a signal and pointed at the beams. Nick lifted his hand into the air, and one of the beams creaked and groaned as it lifted off the rest of the stack.

"You try to get your field underneath the beam," Nick shouted over the noise that was building all around them as other Magnets began their work. "The foreman will show you placement, and you have to get it close enough for Muscle group to slide it into position."

Nick shifted his weight to the left, and Alan watched the beam float in a direct, efficient manner across the lot and onto the concrete foundation the supervisors had been standing on before. Nick then lowered his right arm so that his hands were one on top of the other. The beam then rotated vertically, and Nick slid his arms – and the beam – across the concrete foundation; then a Muscle worker grabbed it with gloved hands and pushed the beam down into holes that were designated for the metal supports.

"See? Easy peasy," Nick exhaled. There was always a certain level of mental exhaustion involved with moving such large objects.

Alan looked back at the beam and saw Marshall's eyes glow white-hot, and a spark ignited at the beam's bottom section, welding it to the foundation's support structure. Everybody had a job - even Castor, who was sulkily cooking pots with his hands – and nobody seemed to care much about who was telling them what to do. Alan figured it couldn't hurt to go with the flow, and let his co-workers lead the way. If people who had been doing this, seemingly for years, then he certainly could swallow his pride and be part of the system too. Even if he was building the next precinct's government processing office.

"Okay, Alan, now I'm going to lift a beam. Now I want you to do the rotation for me. It helps for the higher elevation. Do you think you can handle that?" Nick explained, his voice becoming higher pitched and patronizing.

Nick's eyes were wide, burning into Alan as they waited for him to acknowledge Nick's authority. Alan rolled his eyes and nodded back. Nick turned his back from Alan, and Alan let out a deep sigh.

The next beam screeched as it scraped across the rest of the stack and finally lifted off and came up over their heads. Alan lifted his hands and rotated them like Nick had done before. The beam struggled as it rotated.

"I can take it," Alan shouted back to Nick.

"You're not ready, kid," Nick yelled back over the din of construction chatter.

Alan pushed on Nick's field, wresting control of it from him. Nick could tell what was happening and pushed back. The beam groaned as two forces pushed on it from different angles.

"Knock it off, kid!"

"I can do it," Alan shouted back.

The beam couldn't handle the two forces and as the fields changed angles, the beam spun out of control. Alan watched as the beam fell toward them. Alan and Nick fell to the floor as the support beam came down on top of them. Alan closed his eyes, waiting for the crunch of bones and for his brains to spill out on the ground. But the crunch never came. Alan opened his eyes. Marshall was standing over him; his arms hoisted upward, beam in hand. Marshall was a rare mutation. Alan had heard rumors of multi-mutations, but he'd never met one before.

"Kid, you wanna' move."

Alan slid backward away from the beam's shadow, and Marshall settled the beam back onto the ground.

"What is wrong with you, kid? I told you to let me handle it. You had one simple job, and you couldn't even do that," Nick was yelling in the silence of the moment. Everyone had stopped working for a brief moment to witness the accident, and the silence was now filled with Nick's whining.

"I didn't mean to do it. You could've just let me handle it instead of trying to take control back," Alan justified.

Nick's nostrils flared, and an errant metal rod flew toward Alan's head. A hand jutted out and caught the rebar before it could impale Alan. Marshall held the rod as it strained to reach Alan. Marshall looked sideways at Nick; his eyes glowing.

"You don't want to do this, Nick."

The supervisors were chattering through walkie talkies, and a man clad in black, including black helmet, entered from the gate entrance. He reminded Alan of the military guards at the 305 building, with their covered faces and their forceful commands. Alan could tell that the guard was looking their way. Nick didn't see the man coming towards them. He was too busy thinking about what it would be like to ram a bar through Alan's cranium.

"Stand down, Magnet," the man said in a stern tone.

Nick finally realized he had an audience, but it was too late. Marshall bent the metal bar and began advocating.

"Everything's fine here, officer. Just a little disagreement. Nick is very sorry, and this will never happen again," Marshall said with confidence. "We're sorry to bother you."

The man didn't even look at Marshall. He didn't know the situation, and he didn't care really. There was a zero-tolerance policy for fighting on job sites.

"Nicholas Bradford, you are cited one strike for insubordinate behavior and attempted assault. This is your third strike. Come peacefully," the man stated in a rote, memorized speech.

"It wasn't my fault. That freakin' kid...," Nick whined. The agent lifted his forearm, his fist balled in a fiercely tight grip, and Nick found himself floating in a mad rush toward the officer. It was an ability Alan had never seen before. It wasn't magnetism or strength, but something much scarier. Alan could feel a cold sweat wrapping around his skin and his gut was on fire. The agent pulled specialized restraints from his vest and violently cuffed Nick, wrenching his arms uncontrollably to Nick's back where he was locked in place. The guard pulled a charcoal colored sack from his satchel and pulled it over Nick's face in one frenzied movement.

The agent raised his head from Nick and pointed to Alan among the crowd.

"Alan Mitchell, you are cited one strike for insubordinate behavior. This is your first strike. Cease further insubordinate actions or you will be cited again," the agent rattled off the sentencing efficiently and without emotion. "Please return to your work."

The agent walked out of the work camp in silence. A woman was standing at the front entrance, and, as the gate shut, a piercing blue light blinded the crowd for a brief moment. Then they were gone, the work crew left only to guess where they had vanished. Marshall looked back at Alan, a confusing mixture of disappointment, anger, and compassion lining the wrinkles in his face.

"I'm sorry, Marshall, I didn't know…"

"It happens, kid. Not usually on the first day, but it happens," Marshall sighed, and he picked up Alan's hard hat off the dusty ground, and then placed it back on his head.

Alan looked over and saw Athena standing outside the truck, her hand gripping the back door. Her eyes were wide, her mouth agape; but when she realized Alan was staring at her, she looked away and went back to work.

The rest of the camp went back to their work as well. After a brief scolding from his new supervisor, Alan went back to work with his magnet group. The noise returned - the hushed voices crowding together with the hum of metal beams echoing as they scraped and slammed into place - but all Alan could think about was Nick Bradford, his five-minute-boss, and the inevitable appointment Nick had with the Board.

Alan felt a large knot tug at the anchor in his chest. Everything seemed to blur into the background as everyone carried on with their work, but Alan was left wondering what this place would make of him in the end, and if he would share in Nick's fate soon enough. *One strike on the first day?* The pattern didn't set a great precedent, and Alan was worried that he would soon be with Nick, wherever that might be.

four

Alan didn't eat well at dinner that night. He almost forgot to eat at all. He arrived late to the cafeteria, something that looked transported straight out of Alan's old high school. He thought he escaped that prison, but it was now some new trap.

He stared down the row of cafeteria food, picked over and festering in grease, and felt something gnawing at the pit of his stomach. It was the bottom of the barrel. He scraped a spoonful of sloppy joe meat onto a faded pink tray, cracked plastic from several years of use and ill-repair. He drizzled some cream corn onto another compartment on the tray and called it a complete meal.

Alan left the hallway of lukewarm food, to find a similarly tepid response from a large room with cafeteria tables and a few stragglers pretending to eat what passed for food.

Alan sat down at a long table - a cheap pressboard plank with matching attached benches painted a sickly green hue - and proceeded to poke at his food with a flimsy spork. He sat a long time by himself, poking at the yellow kernels of corn and rolling them around in the sauce. He tapped his spork on the edge of the faded pink tray, his eyes fixated on the slop.

"Hey, kid. I told you not to be late," Marshall quipped, looking down at Alan's food.

Alan looked up as if snapped out of hypnosis. Athena rolled her eyes in a playful manner and opened the foil wrapper around her pudding cup, a rare find that she traded two cigarettes for.

"I was just…," Alan's voice trailed off as his mind gave up on whatever excuse he was trying to conjure.

"I remember my first day on the job too," Marshall joked and slapped Alan on the back, a bit too hard for him. Alan coughed a bit and went back to poking at his food. "It gets better. Well, it gets *easier.*"

"It doesn't," Athena retorted, her eyes on her pudding. "But you can trick yourself for long enough."

"Thanks," Alan replied sarcastically. Athena slowly blinked her eyes and looked up from the pudding.

"I'm just being honest, Alan. This place doesn't change. You change. We all change. Enough to get through another day. Sometimes that's enough."

"Athena," Marshall said, his voice sounding stern and corrective.

Athena shook her head, her fingers tapping against the lunch table pressboard like keys clicking on a typewriter. She drew in a heavy breath and laid into Marshall.

"Marshall, stop patronizing him. He knows what situation we're in. To say otherwise is to treat him like a kid, and he's not. None of us are anymore. We don't have that luxury," Athena spoke in a rush, as if there was no time to take breaths between thoughts, "And don't tell me I'm being pessimistic. I'm a realist. This is the shit we're in, for better or worse."

"Get out of my head, Athena," Marshall replied in a lower tone, his arms against his chest. Athena rolled her eyes and pressed her hands to her throbbing skull.

"I'm not in your head, Marshall. We agreed I wouldn't do that to you. But I've known you long enough to know when we're in for another one of your 'sunshine speeches', and I'm not having it today. Nick was an idiot, but he was *our* idiot. And I know, Alan didn't mean to get him in trouble, but he did."

She was a *Reader.* Alan didn't think to ask before, but now it was right in front of him. Athena could read people's minds. *Could she read his mind too?*

"Only what's on the surface," Athena replied out loud to Alan's thought, and then she exhaled deeply, "But I try not to do it." Athena looked over at Marshall, "*I've been told* it's not polite."

Marshall uncrossed his arms and leaned toward Athena.

"Athena," Marshall said, his voice higher pitched and repentant. Athena pushed herself away from the table with one shaky, violent push.

"Don't worry about it, Marshall. I wasn't that hungry," Athena groaned, looking at her half-eaten pudding cup. Her lips pulled back, a pained smile on her face. "I'm going to take a walk."

Athena left Alan and Marshall alone at the cafeteria table.

"That would've been good to know about Athena," Alan said to Marshall. Alan cleared his throat, his hands pressing the side of his face. "I mean what if…"

"Kid… *Alan,* if Athena wanted to know something about you, she'd figure out how to get it. But she doesn't care. So don't worry about it. I would've told you if it had crossed my mind. Enjoy your dinner."

Marshall got up and walked out of the cafeteria, leaving Alan to stare at congealing cream corn.

~ ~ ~

After dinner, Alan took a walk around the complex, seeing how people kept their rooms. Nothing seemed different from his own stark room. A few people had colorful curtains instead of the drab gray ones that were in his room, but everything else seemed the same. He saw a few guys standing around in one of the doorways, mostly a few guys from the Magnets group. They gave Alan rude glares, so he guessed they were Nick's friends. They dispersed and Alan saw that it was Nick's room they were standing around.

Alan stared at the front of Nick's room, somehow hoping he would just appear in the doorway and punch Alan's lights out. But the doorway was empty. The door was opened, and the room had been stripped of any sense of living. The bathroom light was on, and all Alan could see was a mattress without its sheets. It was as naked as his heart felt.

Back home when Alan ran his mouth or took a joke too far, he'd get popped in the face and that would be it. Now, Alan was responsible for a man being locked up. Well, *more* locked up than he already was.

Alan felt like he was fourteen again, waiting for his parents to come home from a date. But this time they weren't coming home. In fact, they weren't coming back, and they had abandoned Alan in this purgatory between the real world and death.

Alan felt his index fingers scratching at his thumbs. He raised a shaky hand to paw at his hair. His eyes darted from Nick's bathroom sink to the empty dresser to the doorframe to the concrete balcony walkway beneath him. Nothing here was going to be easy. There were no goodbyes. There was seldom a thought as people passed out of existence.

Marshall cleared his throat as he approached Alan. He was on his way back to his room, when he noticed Alan transfixed by Nick's former room.

"You okay, kid?"

Alan felt the color rush out of his face, and he turned back, standing in Nick's room like the ghost that was haunting him.

"Yeah... uh. I'm... fine?" Alan muttered, his voice trailing off in a high pitch.

Marshall turned his body, leaving the doorway open next to him. He motioned for Alan to follow. Alan looked back at the room and thought of the erased man who used to call it home. He looked back at Marshall, who motioned his head in a more pressing fashion. Marshall cleared his throat and held his arm out the door. Alan finally rolled his eyes and gave a half-hearted nod. He followed Marshall back to Alan's room.

"Kid, if you didn't show up to work today... Heck, if you never showed up to our camp ever, someone would've set Nick off; and he'd be seeing the Board anyway. Did you stop to wonder how he got the first two strikes?"

Alan opened his door, but Marshall kept talking.

"Sometimes you can't stop people from doing what they want to do, and sometimes what they want to do is be self-righteous, or angry, or in charge. And you can't fix people if they don't want to be fixed. Nick Bradford had his issues long before you messed with his beam."

Alan sat down on his bed, pulling a bunch of rough cotton blanket into his hand. Marshall leaned on the doorway, and continued talking, regardless of Alan's silence.

"Don't think about how you can control his situation. You don't owe him the patience. I can't count how many times I tried to help Nick; kept him from getting caught, tried to work with him on his temper. He never wanted to get right. He got comfortable being a jerk, and he didn't feel like changing," Marshall explained in calm, controlled sentences, "Now, I don't know where he's gone, but if they just moved him to a new camp; it'll be the same there. If he's not... well, if he's not, then that's on him. He knows the world we live in. You didn't send Nick away, kid. That's just how things are here, and Nick knew that already, and he still chose his path. Now, go to bed before lights out. You already have one strike."

five

"Get up, Mr. Mitch-," Finch's voice was cut short when he peered into Alan's room and saw that he was already up and dressed. "Five minutes."

Alan nodded and grabbed his vest and hat. One week. It was exactly one week since he joined the 308th precinct, and he still didn't sleep well, but not from living arrangements.

No, Alan couldn't sleep because all he could think about was Nick Bradford's horrible fate. He heard some of the magnet crew walking by his room as curfew began the night before. They were talking about Nick, hoping they would see him again. One of the voices shouted, "You idiots, we're not going to see Nick again. They never come back. You see the board; you don't see nobody ever again! So, shut the hell up."

It was deathly silent after that. Alan wondered how long it would last: when would he be hauled away to the Board? He already had one strike, on his first day no less, so it was entirely possible he'd be gone within the month. He looked down at his dresser, the top drawer open and half-full of simple t-shirts. His hand rested on a watch lying on top of his shirts. The watch was from home, a simple weekender styled number with leather strap and analog face. It held two very conflicting memories for Alan, memories that liked to rise to the surface every so often; especially when he looked at the cracked glass on the face.

Alan soon realized he had an audience and looked up. Athena was standing in the doorway, and Marshall jumped out from behind her, as if Alan couldn't see his hulking frame behind Athena. Alan stifled a laugh.

"Hey, Alan, you ready for week two?" Marshall asked enthusiastically. Athena rolled her eyes, her arms crossed and her left shoulder leaned up against the doorway.

"Sure," Alan replied half-heartedly, and he put the watch back in the dresser, trying to push the memories - like the drawer - back out of sight.

"Yes, week two is just week one... again," Athena joked, this time a small crack in her smirk, revealing more humor than cynicism.

"That sounded almost excited, Athena," Marshall said with a big grin, and the three of them walked down to the lobby for week two of Alan's job.

Everything seemed to be marching in rhythm now: same lobby, same people, same bus, same route, same site. It was all a matter of routine, and it gave Alan time to ponder how his week had been.

Another day, another beam. Alan tried to pretend he didn't notice the rest of the Magnet group giving him the evil eye as they began working. He couldn't blame them. Nick was gone. He was the type of gone that nobody really understood until they lived it. Nick was an unperson. Nobody mentioned him in roll call. The supervisors acted as if he'd never existed. Save for a few sparse remarks from his coworkers, Nick was little more than a fading memory to workers of 308. Alan had ruminated on this fact the entire week and had come to a conclusion: never again.

Alan decided at some point in his sleep-elusive nights that he was going to be different. If this was the hand he'd been dealt, then he would be as safe as possible. It was one thing getting yourself in trouble; getting someone else in trouble was another thing entirely.

"Never again," Alan mouthed to himself as he lifted his hand and played support to one of the other Magnet crew members. He was going to make sure he never got someone a strike again, and he was going to honor Nick by playing by the rules.

~ ~ ~

The lunch bell rang out, echoing in the open air of the construction yard. Alan joined Marshall in line outside the food truck, where the groups were receiving their chicken or bean tacos. At least, Alan assumed it was chicken. Castor was standing next to Athena, his face hovering over a cauldron filled with meat ingredient. Alan could see the dead eyes; he knew that look.

"Chicken or bean?" Athena asked Alan.

"Um... what would you recommend?" Alan asked with a toothy smile, an eyebrow raised.

Athena made a half-smile and looked at the two options. Castor was pulling a ladle up and down, the soupy brown mush of the beans drizzling out. Athena's stomach turned for a moment, and she looked back at Alan. "I think I'd go with chicken."

"Then chicken it is," Alan said, his voice slightly more optimistic than it had been all day. His eyes then reluctantly moved over to Castor, who was none-too-happy to see the newbie giving him requests. Castor rolled his eyes and prepared some tacos; then he placed them in a paper box on top of some Spanish rice. Alan smiled at Athena - who smiled back - and Alan took his meal back to the picnic tables adjacent to the concrete foundation of their construction site.

Alan looked down and saw oozing refried beans cascading down his tortillas and onto his rice. Alan let out a deep, frustrated sigh.

"Castor," Alan clenched his teeth, his emotions pitching toward anger.

"Didn't you order chicken?" Marshall asked with a big grin, and he set his tray down on the table next to Alan.

"I thought so. It was all a blur," Alan replied in a sour tone.

"I figured as much. Here," Marshall put his plate in front of Alan. They sure were chicken-esque tacos. "I actually like bean tacos. Everybody thinks I'm nuts, Athena included."

"She seems to think that about you in general," Alan joked.

"Oh, look at that. New guy's got jokes," Marshall smiled. "Good to see you getting acclimated. Yeah, Athena thinks I'm crazy in general, but aren't we all a little crazy?"

Alan thought about it for a minute. Marshall had a point. Everyone seemed to be on the verge of antisocial aggression, save for Marshall. It didn't take much effort to push Nick over the edge toward homicidal behavior. Castor almost melted Finch's arm off over a seemingly insignificant slight. Athena had bitten Marshall's head off at dinner merely because Marshall was trying to be positive with his outlook.

"Yeah, everybody seems crazy here. Everybody except for you, Marshall," Alan said, and he took a bite of his chicken taco.

"What're you talking about, kid? I'm the craziest one here," Marshall fired back, his face lacking the trademark smile Alan had grown accustomed to.

"Everyone here is looking for a reason to start a fight, and you just try to keep us sane. What makes you crazy like us?"

"Because, kid," Marshall replied, and he looked down apathetically at his meal. He stuck a fork in his rice and cleared his throat. He locked eyes with Alan, and, suddenly, he appeared far older than Alan had considered before.

"I chose to be here."

~ ~ ~

The next day was much the same: another sleepless night, more bossy supervisors, more beam placement, and a really sore back from standing around all day.

Alan groaned as his body slumped down into one of the lawn chairs out in the courtyard. Several of the other workers - George, Marshall, Athena, a woman named Lara, and Castor - were with Alan sitting around a small foldout table. Everyone but Athena had playing cards in their hands, with a pool of random odds and ends in the center of the table. Loose cigarettes, bubble gum in foil sticks, one blue macaroni and cheese box, and a pair of new tube socks.

"I take it Athena isn't allowed to play," Alan joked.

"And talkative little bitches," Castor interjected, his eyes still locked in on his cards, which were shit as usual.

Athena's mirthy smile broke open around her caramel lips as she responded to Alan's question. "Yes, I'm not allowed to play. I've been told I cheat. But I've yet to see any credible evidence."

Athena turned her gaze to Marshall who was still agonizing over his pair of twos and the loose bubble gum sticks piled up around his elbows. Athena cleared her throat and Marshall looked up from his cards. He looked back down at his cards and answered in a bored monotone.

"It is guilty until proven innocent in poker," Marshall replied and then raised his voice as if reading off some grand prologue to a fantasy epic, "Prove your innocence and you can enter to win this vast treasure."

"I'd rather watch you morons try to win with a pair of twos, a suicide king, and two cards short of a straight. And, George, you're never going to get that second Ace," Athena said in a dry tone. Everyone at the table threw their cards down in unison and groaned Athena's name as loud as possible.

"Seriously, what the hell, Athena?" Castor shouted. "I'm going back to my room. You nerds can eat it."

Castor pulled back from the table and went upstairs with what little winnings he had left. Alan, eyes wide and lips curled downward, looked around at the rest of the group.

"Eat *what*?" Alan asked.

"I'm not sure Castor even knows," Marshall replied.

"I *know* he doesn't," Athena joked through squinting eyes and a big smile.

The group chortled, and Marshall pulled all the cards together into a pile and stacked them up. If they lost anymore cards, they'd be hard pressed to put a straight together. Not that anyone ever really got anything that good to begin with.

"Who wins the pot?" Alan asked.

Athena looked down at the pile of loose junk sitting at the center of the table. "Is it really *winning*? I mean haven't we won the lottery already?"

Athena raised her arms, motioning to the courtyard around them. George and Lara chuckled, and George grabbed one of the cigarettes from the pile and handed it to Lara who lit it immediately with her fingers. Marshall grabbed the box of macaroni and cheese before anyone else could. Alan raised an eyebrow at him.

"What? I like mac and cheese," Marshall said defensively. "It's the little things."

"I've heard we have limited choices at the market, but that stuff has to be passed expiration," Alan pointed at the blue box in Marshall's hands.

Marshall looked down at the battered box. "Mac doesn't go bad, Alan. Just crunchier. Besides, you can never find them at the market. When Castor put it down on the table, I knew it was my lucky day."

Lara took a drag off her cigarette and let the smoke spill out of her mouth in trails. "Never seen a man so overcome by pasta shells and cheese dust."

"It's the little things," Marshall acknowledged, shaking the box around to hear the melodious cascade of dried pasta. He nodded in Lara's direction. "There is not a lot to savor here, but at least I can get my mac and cheese."

Alan recalled what Marshall admitted to him earlier in the day. Marshall was here voluntarily. His admission now sat in Alan's mind, festering in every conversation they had. It was hard to bear the tension.

Alan got up from the table and went back into the lobby where Finch was sitting at his desk watching the news play on a TV attached to the adjacent corner walls.

"This is not a time to be soft, Senator. Our very way of life is in jeopardy because of these individuals. Incarceration is the last of our worries," the guest replied to the other show's guest, a Senator from Oregon. The Senator was older, perhaps in her early fifties with graying hair, light skin and rosy cheeks. Her eyes squinted at the other guest's remarks.

"Forgive me if I don't see how these people should forfeit the rights we all hold so dear just because they were born different from us," the Senator responded. "Do we represent freedom for all, or just for those we want?"

"Senator, we can't afford the luxury of freedom for individuals who represent an existential threat to us. They could upend the fabric of society!" the man raised his voice, and the moderator intervened.

"It seems that we still have a lot to talk about, so we'll return after these important messages…"

A commercial came on for a local politician. It started with a black and white photo of a smiling candidate and was interrupted by a voice over a man with a low, ominous tone.

"Senator Randall Marks put your children in danger by allowing genetic deviants to remain in your schools all across the state and made your tax dollars pay for it. This is not America. This is not California. This election day, say no to Senator Randall Marks."

Finch flipped the channel to local sports and clapped the remote back down on his desk.

"Something I can do for you, Mr. Mitchell?" Finch asked, without looking up from his paperwork.

"No, nothing I can think of. Just thought I'd hear what was going on in the world."

"Best to keep it out of your mind. Nothing either of us can do about it anyways," Finch responded, and then he rubber stamped a document with a loud thud. Finch looked down at the names on the triplicate sheets, then cleared his itchy throat and ripped off the bottom copy and stuffed it into a red folder that then went into a filing cabinet. Finch slammed the filing cabinet drawer shut and looked back at Alan.

"We have an early morning tomorrow, Mr. Mitchell. Please, just go to your room, and leave me in peace. I don't want to add any more names to the sheets tonight."

Alan could feel his chest tense up. His eyes traveled from Finch's eyes down to the pink sheets sitting on Finch's desk. The bold heading jumped out from the page: Request for Removal. Everyone who got three strikes off the clock ended up as a name on a sheet and shipped out the next day. Poof.

Alan looked past the header: a list of names and serial numbers. Alan scanned it quickly. He saw a G and L name with serials.

"George and Lara?" Alan didn't realize he said the names out loud.

"Mr. Mitchell," Finch interjected. "I'm not interested in this right now. It's been a shit day, and tomorrow's going to be a. Shit. day. Just go to your room and thank your God in heaven that your name isn't on this list."

six

"Alan!" Athena's voice echoed inside Alan's brain, ping-ponging its way between his ear drums.

Alan was dazing at a box of cereal turned backwards on a rickety metal shelf in the old, repurposed grocery store. His eyes strayed away from the cartoon characters making fiber and iron puns to look at Athena, who was standing next to him in the aisle.

Alan couldn't remember the last time he saw such a terrible grocery store. There wasn't produce or meat; really, anything fresh was lacking. Alan looked back at the box of cereal, the date marked way past its expiration.

"Get out of your head, Alan. We don't have much time left to get stuff before curfew," Athena coaxed.

But Alan couldn't get out of his head because he was still conflicted about what Marshall told him earlier at work. How could someone pick this life for themselves voluntarily? Alan contemplated that some special form of madness was constricting Marshall, pressing him into compulsory labor.

Alan gritted his teeth and picked up the dented cereal box. The faded orange box sported five different kinds of oats. Five, stale kinds of oats.

"You get out of my head," Alan chided, his eyes slowly turning back to look at her. He smirked and tipped the box of cereal at Athena.

"I'm not, but don't give me any ideas," Athena said with an innocent smile.

Alan didn't wait for her to finish and changed the subject to something that was bothering him.

"When Marshall said we were going to a grocery store, I thought maybe it would have... *groceries*," Alan said with a grin and a raised eyebrow. Athena gave a short chuckle and looked at their aisle, sparsely filled with mostly boxed cereals and snack foods. The aisles to either side were also comprised of mostly canned foods and other snack foods that lasted a long time.

"Yeah, and they don't replenish the stock very often. Just don't lose your toothpaste. Trust me."

"Oh, was I supposed to be brushing my teeth?" Alan joked, and he shook up the box of cereal. Athena punched Alan in the arm playfully. Alan feigned a groan of pain at her fist, cereal shaking around in its box. He sucked a breath in through clenched teeth and gasped.

"Stop!" Athena laughed, and she put Alan's box of cereal back onto the shelf. "And you don't want that. Especially if you won't be brushing your teeth for the foreseeable future. It'll rot them right out, and we can't ruin that cute smile, can we?"

"*Cute* smile?" Alan questioned, his smile ear to ear. Athena felt the blood rush to her reddening face. What seemed like an hour was merely a few seconds before Marshall came jogging into the aisle with a basket full of mac and cheese boxes.

"Guys! Mac! They have mac finally!" Marshall showed them his haul, his outstretched hands holding up a plastic orange basket filled with an odd assortment of blue boxes with macaroni scrawled in elegant cursive. They rattled as he shook the basket, enthralled with his find. "They never have mac and cheese. This is the best day."

Alan was still taken aback by Marshall's revelation early, and now he was aghast that Marshall hardly seemed to care or remember what they had talked about before. Alan didn't realize he was giving Marshall a weird look until he noticed Marshall giving him the same look back. Athena had been talking in the void of conversation about missing chocolate, specifically dark chocolate in squares, when she noticed the two men were exchanging glances.

"Do I need to give you two a minute?" Athena asked, a box of shells and cheese in one hand and her other hand outstretched to the boys. Alan and Marshall looked at each other, not sure what the other was thinking. The one who could read minds didn't much feel like doing it, and she was losing her patience with the deaf and mute routine.

"I can go back to the bus. Nothing looks good to me anyway," Athena motioned to the entrance where the bus, and most of the crew, were waiting. Alan nodded. It seemed like the only thing his mind could do. Athena grabbed a box of cereal, a raisin and bran type, and dropped it into Alan's basket.

"That's the stupid tax, I'll see you two boys back at the bus."

Athena walked out the door, the doorway bell chiming as she exited. Marshall looked down at the bran distastefully, his top lip curling up on the right side of his face.

"That looks like crap-," Marshall started, but Alan cut him off mid-sentence.

"Are we going to talk about your little reveal earlier? Or are you just going to leave it at, 'I chose to be here'?"

Marshall cleared his throat. It was a slip up, plain and simple. He'd gotten too comfortable with Alan. Alan had this way of smiling, listening, that made a person want to tell things - secrets - that weren't meant to be shared.

"Listen, kid, don't take my words and make them more than what they were," Marshall said plainly, "I spoke out of turn, and I don't want you to take what I said as some deep, dark secret to fill up the hours of your mundane workday. Let's just leave it at that. It's nothing. It's not important to you."

"Fine," Alan replied, stone-faced but annoyed. "I'll pretend I never heard it. Let's get out of here."

Marshall didn't believe Alan was going to give up that easily, but he did know that the bus was about to leave without them, so it didn't bother him much to leave it where it was for the time being. The two checked out, when the store manager and their supervisor, Mr. Finch walked up with Athena. They motioned for Alan to follow. Alan grabbed the backpack out of his basket and they were led outside.

Around the corner, the store's white brick had been defaced. Alan pulled up on the shoulder strap of his backpack. The paint was still dripping, trails of red spray paint rolling down the wall's brick facade. It was in big, messy capital letters: *FREAKS*.

Alan sighed; his eyes transfixed on the graffiti. Finch, Athena, and the manager were all looking at him. The manager pulled a bucket up and pulled the mop that was leaning up against the wall to his chest. He handed Alan the mop and slid the bucket across the sidewalk to him, a splash of water sloshing out onto the asphalt. Athena picked up a paint brush, white paint already slathered across its bristled tips.

"So...?" Alan's voice trailed off, a confused look on his face.

"Clean this up. Can't have our store so messy," Finch grunted, a wisp of his hair getting loose. He tightly packed it back into his limited hair.

"I didn't...," Alan grumbled.

The manager cleared his throat. "We don't care, kid. Just clean this crap up. Unless, of course, you'd like another strike."

Alan's upper lip flinched, his eyebrows slanting at the callous way the manager threw strikes around. Those weren't tokens for some prize. They were tickets to hell. The manager squinted back at

Alan, fished in his pocket for his keys, and strolled back over to the entrance.

"Let's just get to it," Athena sighed, and she picked up a bristled brush that was sitting next to the bucket.

Finch followed the manager, their talk of some recent sporting event echoing down the street, filled with boisterous trash talk and laughter. Alan slid the backpack down his arm and onto the sidewalk, then pushed the mop into the bucket of cold water, hearing the gulp and splurt as the mop soaked in the moisture. He pulled the mop out and slapped it against the wall, sending water into the air. Athena jumped back from the spray.

"Jeez, Alan. Watch what you're doing," Athena complained, and she rubbed the water off her arms.

"I'm well aware of what I'm doing," Alan groaned. "Cleaning up after people who hate us."

"*Hate* is a strong word," Athena remarked, and she wiped off the excess water and started painting the wall where Alan had mopped.

"Yes," Alan replied, "It is."

~ ~ ~

65

After scrubbing the wall, Alan and Athena got back on the bus that would take them back to their dorms. The bus was full, and people were chatting as the sun sat leisurely right above its final rest for the night. The orange light cast a line across the horizon as the bus made its way back to the 308's compound.

Athena was telling Alan about her old cat. If the stories were true, her cat was the smelliest cat in all the world. In fact, at one point, Athena mistook him for garbage in the middle of the night. She tried to put him in the can, but as soon as she had grabbed the tail, all hell broke loose. Alan laughed all the way through the riotous tale of the smelliest cat, and so did Athena.

"Do you have stories from back home, Alan?" Athena asked. Alan smiled.

"Yeah, I have stories. I mean, I had a childhood, Athena," Alan said jokingly.

"Sometimes we forget," Athena replied, her eyes looking out at the sun setting. "It can be easier that way… But who would want to forget about your garbage cat?"

Athena smiled brightly, a smile Alan didn't recognize. Maybe it was the smile Athena wanted to share, or the one she never would. When she realized Alan was looking at her, she stopped immediately.

"Your turn. Tell me a story," Athena said. Alan turned his body toward her and looked in her green eyes. He remembered this one time...

"Who's Molly?" Athena asked quizzically.

Alan wasn't sure what happened first: the swerve or the collision. Either way the bus that was carrying them swiped a car and slid against a railing on the road back to the compound. Sparks flew through the air, and people screamed. But not Alan. He'd witnessed this before.

The bus was careening toward a large tree at over sixty miles per hour. Alan stood up in the aisle and held his hand out, causing the air brakes to screech from the overload. Alan felt the front of the truck: the metal fender, the wheels, the frame. He felt its pulse, the magnetic field. He pressed his mind as far as it could go. The bus groaned to a halt, not three inches from the massive old tree.

The bus passengers all seemed to exhale at the same time. Alan didn't look at his friends, but at the other vehicle smoking down the road. Alan ran out of the bus wreck and across the street to the small sedan bent up against the railing.

DMP buses were programmed to avoid human vehicles at all costs, even at the expense of the bus and its occupants. But another car could strike a DMP bus if it lost control *or if someone really wanted to hit it.*

Alan looked down at the woman slumped over in the sedan, a bloody airbag ballooned up against her face. Her long brown hair was scattered in strands around the bag, mixed with blood and fragments of the steering wheel. The blood in Alan's veins ran cold, and he could perceive some of it ran out as well. His arm throbbed, bathed in dark blood in the early moonlight.

Molly.

Alan tried to forget. He thought serving his time would dull the memories. But even now she was on the surface, easy enough for Athena to pluck the name out of the air.

"Alan," it was Athena, standing a few feet away, between Alan and the bus. Alan felt a shiver down his spine, his hairs on his arms standing up. His arm hurt like hell, now that the shock was wearing off.

"Is everybody okay?" Alan asked.

"More or less."

Alan didn't look back, his eyes still set on the woman in the car. She didn't look much older than twenty, a bottle of alcohol propped up in her dashboard, broken in half.

"Why would she-?" Alan managed to grumble out of his mouth, his throat hoarse and tight. Inside the compound, outside the compound, nothing felt real anymore. Everything was some grand illusion of reality. Everything until this.

"- drink?" Athena finished the sentence.

Alan clenched his teeth. Senseless was what it was. Free, not free. Everybody was somehow in prisons of their own. Alan mused that whether he had gone to the 308 or not, he'd still be locked away in some respect. Like the woman who drank until she couldn't have the sense to keep on the road, Alan would've dulled his memories some other way.

Sirens faintly skipped across the hills in the distance, the red and blue lights of the police heading their way. They would soon be back in the compound, left wondering what had really transpired out on the road that evening. The only person who knew the truth would never speak again.

"Alan," Athena spoke up, her voice shaky. Alan looked back at Athena. Her eyes wouldn't even blink, their attention intently focused on Alan's face. Something in them seemed to know the answer to what she was about to ask, but she'd ask it again anyway.

"Alan," Athena asked, wringing cold sweat in her hands, "Who's Molly?"

seven

F inch had everyone in the lobby with the Healer EMT
division in attendance to treat the wounded from the bus
crash. Alan watched as the break in his arm snapped back into
place and the cuts in his arms sewed shut as if by some invisible
magic. The person who was helping him, a dispassionate blonde-
haired man in his late thirties, ran his hands across Alan's arm
then held up one to Alan's face. The cut in Alan's eyebrow sealed.

"Thanks, *Linus*," Alan said, peering down at the man's nametag
briefly. The man - with no emotion whatsoever - nodded and
motioned for Alan to step out of line.

Finch continued to yell out in the lobby, "When you are finished,
head straight to your room! Do not stop to talk! It is lights out!
We're not on vacation! We have work tomorrow! If you lost your
groceries, you will have to file the proper paperwork! Go to bed!"

"Alan," Athena called out to Alan, as he tried to get through the
crowd and into the courtyard.

Alan swallowed the lump in his throat and pressed his way through the sea of bodies, glancing back quickly at Athena who also struggling to make her way to the courtyard. He pushed harder, finding people were beginning to yield to his impatience and frantic pace.

The crowd seemed to reform as a barrier between Athena and Alan. Athena looked over at Marshall who was handling the flow of people back to the courtyard. She gave him an annoyed look, and he stepped over to her.

"Pardon me. Okay. Ahem, sorry about that. Pardon me. And Pardon my reach," Marshall wiggled between people, then grabbed a few coworkers blocking Athena and lifted them out of the way. "There we go."

"Thanks, Marshall," Athena said as she ran past him.

~ ~ ~

"Alan!" Athena's voice was muffled from inside Alan's room. "Alan, open the door."

Alan didn't answer. He just sat in stunned silence.

"Alan, please, I'm sorry," Athena pleaded, her forehead pressed against the door. It wasn't locked, but she didn't want to push any further than she already had. "Come on, just open the door."

No answer.

Marshall walked up behind Athena and motioned for her to go. He knocked on the door, then opened it without waiting for a response.

It was dark in Alan's room. The only visibility was from the fluorescent lighting outside in the hall, peeking in through the window. Alan sat with his back up against the dresser in his room. His right hand was holding the broken watch, gliding his thumb back and forth across the cracked glass.

Alan barely acknowledged Marshall's existence. He was *elsewhere*. Marshall paused for a moment, looking at the young man against the dresser. He pressed fingers against his strained eyes, and then inhaled a deep breath.

"Hey, kid," Marshall exhaled in a groaning bellow as he sat down next to Alan against the dresser. He wrapped his arms around his knees and waited in the silence. Several moments passed. "Your arm looks better."

Alan stared ahead at his twin bed. He had been perfectly fine doing his time, going through the motions, clocking in and out. Maybe it would've helped him forget her.

Molly.

"Kid, you seem out of sorts," Marshall sighed. "And that has Athena worried, and she's useless when she's worried."

No answer.

Marshall groaned and got up off of the floor, his shoes leaving a mud stain in the grotesque carpet. Everything felt tight. Arms. Legs. Lungs. Marshall cracked his fingers together and ran a finger across an itch on his eyebrow. He looked at the exit.

"Try to get some sleep, kid. We've got work tomorrow."

Marshall stepped toward the doorway.

"Have you ever seen someone die, Marshall? I mean, really see them. Not like at funeral… but right then… when it happened. Did you see the woman on the road?"

Marshall shook his head, leaning into the doorway.

"I didn't. I was…," Marshall's voice trailed off as he noticed Alan still wasn't making eye contact. Alan looked down at the watch.

"I don't understand it," Alan murmured.

"What's there to understand? Drank too much and did something stupid," Marshall shrugged, then he pushed his hands into his jeans' pockets.

"I can relate," Alan said under his breath. "Not the drinking, per se, but I know stupid."

"I think we all can relate," Marshall replied.

Finch's voice echoed in the hallway for lights out. Marshall stood tall in the doorway.

"This isn't about that girl on the road tonight," Marshall said with a grim expression on his face. "What's with the watch, Alan?"

Alan blinked slowly, and looked down at his broken watch, thumb still sliding across the imperfect, cracked surface.

"It's lights out," Alan replied gravely.

Marshall walked over and sat down on the bed opposite Alan, folding his arms and awaiting Alan's response.

"You think I'm scared of them?"

"You're scared of something," Alan replied, his voice filled with bitterness, and he finally looked up at Marshall.

"That's fair," Marshall cleared his throat. "I can't make you tell me if you don't want to, but eventually you're going to realize we're the only friends you have, kid. That life you had before - the people you knew - they're gone, and they aren't coming back."

Alan clenched his jaw. "I know."

"I used to think I'd get out one of these days. I'd do my time, and they'd just let me go when they lost use for me. But that's not how this works. I made a choice to be here, and that is irreversible. There's no going back to the way things were for me. Same as you."

Marshall's honesty was sobering; sobering in a mood that was already hurtling toward depression. Alan looked back at his broken watch, the last vestige of his time in the real world.

"I remember the day Molly gave me this watch. She had this way of joking about you and you didn't even care. She said to me, 'I got you this watch so you'll stop being late to pick me up.'," Alan laughed. "I've never been the punctual type. Anyway, I was 17, and she was trying to whip me into shape. I took the hint. Hardly ever forgot that watch, and maybe I showed up on time more often. I don't remember. I don't think she really cared all that much about that."

Marshall sat down next to Alan.

"Athena was asking me about a funny story early tonight, and it just reminded me of this one time... Molly's dog - the little guy was a handful - and he liked to jump at the door in her parent's old shed. She kept him in there on cold nights. Well he would just scratch up the door when I came over... all the time. So, one night when I pulled up to her house, I heard Ralph - the dog's name was Ralph if you could believe it - and he was running toward the shed door. So, I just reached out," Alan held his hand out to pantomime his story, "and the door flies open just in time for Ralph to come rolling out into the yard. Dog rolled for probably a good few seconds - felt like minutes - and then Ralph hopped back up and gave me the most confused look. One ear bent down, the other standing straight up like an antenna. He sneezed and dirt came out of his nose. It was hilarious."

Marshall and Alan laughed at the story. Alan laughed so hard there were genuine tears in his eyes. He cleared his throat and continued.

"Course, Ralph was fine. He was a resilient booger, tongue wagging and jumping at my car after that. Molly rolled her eyes at me, and put Ralph back up and we went out for the night. I guess

Athena reminded me that little memories could still be happy memories if you let them."

Marshall nodded.

"How'd your watch break?" Marshall asked, his head tipping in its direction. Alan looked at his broken watch face, his smile evaporating.

"Some memories will *never* be happy memories," Alan murmured and wiped the tears of joy from his eyes.

"How'd the watch break, Alan?"

"Why'd you volunteer for this job?" Alan sneered back at Marshall.

"Touché," Marshall sighed. Alan could see Marshall was struggling with his thoughts. "I'll tell you one thing - one thing - if you tell me about the watch."

Alan groaned and handed the watch to Marshall. Marshall looked at the face, the cracked glass. The hands were forever stuck at one point in time.

2:37. The box showed AM.

"It was late. We were driving home from a party. Raining cats and dogs. Low visibility."

~ ~ ~

Alan smiled at Molly, a fleeting glance away from the road as their car made its way through the torrential downpour. They were supposed to leave the party hours ago, but it was two in the morning, and they were out in the middle of it. Molly smiled uneasily, a tense feeling rattling throughout her body.

"I know, I know. We should've left earlier."

"I didn't say anything," Molly said, a faint veneer of humor laid over her uneasiness.

"Yeah, but you were thinking it," Alan joked, his eyes staring intensely through the windshield.

The wipers were trying their hardest, but there was too much rain. The road was covered in a layer of water, and any little change of the steering wheel created in a volatile movement one way or the other across the road.

Alan tried to fix the defroster on his dashboard. He hadn't noticed the lights growing larger up ahead. Molly sucked in a panicked breath, and Alan looked up. The car was spinning out of control, hydroplaning toward them, and there was no time to respond. Alan threw his hands on the dashboard as a snap reaction. Their car wrenched to the left. The other vehicle smashed into the passenger side of their car, and Alan's head smacked into the steering wheel. Everything went black.

The world was blurry when Alan came to. Alan lifted his head, a nauseous feeling slowly fermenting in his gut. He was on a red stretcher, elevated over the deluge. Flashlights kept dancing over his field of view, and emergency workers passed over him as they worked. Alan couldn't move his head, so his eyes tracked as far to his right as he could. He could see Molly in her own stretcher, as one of the emergency workers zipped her up into a black bag.

Alan couldn't tell if it was the rain in his face or not, but he could feel warm tears trailing down his face as he looked back up into the blinding flashlights.

"Get him to the hospital, the crew will handle the rest of the cleanup. The other driver is paralyzed. Code the woman."

~ ~ ~

"Damn, kid."

Alan took the watch back and held it to his ear. "Hasn't worked ever since."

80

"You know it's not your fault she died, right?"

"Oh, I know… 'it was an accident', 'you didn't mean to'…," Alan trailed off, his face disgusted. "It happened, and if I had just let that stupid idiot hit me, Molly would be alive, and I wouldn't be lifting metal beams in this chain gang for the rest of my life."

"Maybe, but you weren't the one who caused the accident. You just had to react. That's all we can do: react."

"Is that why you ended up in here? You reacted?"

"I was worried about my family," Marshall replied in defense, "It was the best I could do in the situation. If I gave myself up, they had no reason to look for them. You do crazy things for your family."

"That's funny: my folks sold me out," Alan said with a wry smile. "Came home one day from my job, and there was a squad car in our driveway. Parents were standing out on the porch with the officers. No real sense of loss for them. I guess I wasn't lucky enough to have a Marshall in the family."

The room was silent for a few moments. Marshall wasn't sure how much more he wanted to share with Alan. He decided to go for it.

"My siblings are special like us. When the government started rounding us up, we went into hiding, but it didn't last long. We slipped up, and the Board tracked us down to a remote location. If I didn't turn myself in, they would've found my family. It's worth it just knowing they're safe now."

"I was an only child. I guess if I had siblings, I would understand."

"You understand, kid. It's why you wanted to take Molly's place. It's love. Maybe not the same kind of love, but still love."

eight

The next day at the construction site was strange for Alan. Everyone knew that he stopped the bus from smashing into the tree, and they were all alive because he did. Even Castor was on his best behavior. He still jeered at Alan from time to time, but it had less bite to it than usual. Castor handed Alan a warm cup of coffee.

"Here you go, kid. Don't say I never gave you nothin'," Castor cleared his throat, and Alan started walking away. "Now get to work, hero. This doesn't mean I like you!"

The comment felt nice enough - if not for Castor's sarcastic 'hero' quip - so Alan took a sip of coffee and enjoyed what seemed like a luxury around the construction site.

"Nice. Coffee," Marshall said as Alan came up to the crowd waiting for work. "Enjoying the hero perks, I see."

Alan shrugged. "I didn't do anything you guys wouldn't have."

"But you did do it. That takes guts…"

"Or - you know - a lot of stupidity," Athena joked, as she walked past them to the food truck. She called out to Alan, "But we're thankful all the same."

Work seemed to fly by. Everything was blurry and loud, beams being welded into place and slamming into place with ferocity.

A supervisor's whistle sounded in the site, and everyone stopped working. At first Alan though maybe someone had gotten hurt, so he looked around with piercing eyes for the source of trouble. But the real reason for the stoppage was much worse.

Alan could see some commotion at the front gate. A couple of Board operators were talking with one of the supervisors, then the supervisor pointed at Alan. Alan felt the blood in his veins run cold, a hard pit in his stomach.

"Alan Mitchell, stand down," one of the operators shouted, his finger pointing through the crowd, and it parted as he walked to clear the distance.

Everyone parted. Everyone except for Castor. Castor was cleaning up the picnic tables where people had left their snacks and had stopped when all the commotion had interrupted his work. He was livid with the operator.

"What the hell do you think you're doing?" Castor asked as loudly as he could, his voice echoing across the construction site. It filled the deathly silence being created by everyone else. Alan could've sworn he heard hundreds of nervous heartbeats.

"Alan Mitchell, come with us immediately."

"Are you punishing him for saving us? That's messed up, man," Castor replied, his arms folded over his chest. "Says a lot about what you think of us. You know you're one of us, right? You'll never be one of *them* by selling us out."

The operator looked past Castor, his jaw clenching in an effort to keep his composure.

"Alan Mitchell, stand down," the operator replied, "Don't make me say it again."

"Castor, it's okay," Alan called out and started walking forward, but Castor wasn't having any of it.

"I'm not moving, man. This is stupid, and you know it," Castor said in an antagonistic tone. The operator rolled his eyes, and shoved Castor out of the way with a flick of his hand and a thought in his telekinetic head. Castor slammed into the half-constructed building, and his body slumped to the concrete floor.

"Come with me, Mr. Mitchell," the operator said calmly, and then turned to his partner. "Gerry, grab the other one. Insubordination to an operator. Automatic three strikes."

The other operator, Gerry, picked up Castor in one hand, and the four of them walked back to a young woman waiting at the gate.

"Prepare for exfiltration," the operator ordered in his calm tone.

There was another operator at the gate, a woman. She nodded, and held a hand out in front of them. A blue pool of energy spiraled into being, and the operators pushed Alan into it.

Alan felt like he was being stretched apart at his extremities, his arms and legs pulled to their farthest reaches. Then it all imploded, scrunching together at the center of himself.

Alan was blinded by a white light, but, as he acclimated, he realized he was kneeling in a white room. The room appeared almost seamless, a round structure with no corner and no visible door. The operator picked him up by the arm and pulled Alan into a standing position.

"Move," the operator commanded forcefully, wrenching Alan forward and onto his feet.

A doorway appeared in the white room, a piece of the wall sliding away, disappearing into the curve of the round space. They entered a hallway, with metal grated floors and solid white walls. Alan looked up at the ceilings, which were long light panels illuminating the bright hall.

"Tax dollars at work, I see," Alan said sarcastically, and the operator shoved him forward.

"Shut up."

Alan looked over and saw Castor was still knocked out, his body slumped over and bobbing in Gerry's arms as they walked. He recalled how intimidated he was of Castor at the beginning, and to see him carried like a child was chilling.

"I'll take this one to the holding area. Don't wait on me for the Board meeting."

The operator acknowledged Gerry, and pressed Alan further down the hall, as Gerry branched off to the left with Castor's limp body in tow. Alan looked up and committed Castor's hallway number to memory: A5.

A dark amusement came over Alan as he realized that memorizing a hallway number wouldn't mean much since he would never escape. He heard the stories. No one ever came back from the

Board meeting. Now he knew where they went, and it was still as mysterious as it had been before. White halls with metal floors. Seamless disappearing doorways. Long hallways filled with light. No shadows to retreat into. Cameras everywhere, no doubt. Alan's scattered mind catalogued all of these observations for a future opportunity that would never come.

The hallway appeared to end in nothing, but Alan soon realized that a doorway would present itself with proximity to the operators' footsteps. Perhaps the operator wore something that alerted the doors to part? Alan shook his head at the sheer lunacy of his thoughts. What good would it do him to figure out their systems? He was, now more than ever, a prisoner.

As if on cue, the doorway opened itself in front of them in the hall, and they entered in an expansive round room yet again. There was a small table before them with a single chair, and beyond it was an elevated crescent-shaped desk with five chairs where his tribunal would sit and cast judgment.

"Sit down."

"But where will you sit?" Alan joked as he motioned to the empty space around his chair. The operator slammed Alan down onto the chair.

"Shut. up."

"Touchy," Alan replied under his breath, his eyes rolling in their place. Yet another room without doorways, curved in porcelain majesty. Alan would've guessed they were in heaven, if not for the stark lighting and the clear sense that he was about to be punished judiciously and without mercy.

A doorway to his right appeared, and four individuals entered. Two men and two women. They were older, possibly in their late thirties or early forties. One man wore a military uniform while the rest were dressed in business attire, no doubt politicians of some sort. They all carried themselves with a sense of complete boredom. The women had tense faces and tightened lips. The men clenched their jaws and fidgeted with their jackets as they walked. Alan imagined he had pulled a number at the supermarket and was just another number for them to serve a sentence.

The man in the military outfit, sat first and fixed his puffing green uniform. As the others sat down, the military man handed down file folders to the woman next to him, a blonde woman who then handed the leftover papers to the man next to her on the other side of the empty center seat. The spectacled Black man passed the last file to a Latina woman with black hair and deep-set eyes.

The four shuffled the papers in unison and looked down at Alan's file.

"Alan Mitchell," the military officer said Alan's name as if seeing it for the first time. His eyes scanned the paper in front of him. He cleared his throat and looked up at Alan. "You are charged with reckless endangerment of the public, destruction of government property, genetic perjury, insubordination, and cross-contamination of a crime scene. How do you plea?"

"Genetic perjury - wha-?" Alan looked around, but no member of the Board seemed to be giving his response much notice, and they continued the process.

"How do you plea?" the blonde woman asked again impatiently, her tightly pulled-back ponytail waving behind her head. Alan swallowed the lump in his throat and looked at the other members of the Board. The center chair was mysteriously empty.

"Mr. Mitchell, this is really more of a formality," the man in the glasses spoke up, moving his glasses back up onto the bridge of his nose. "We have evidence of these crimes. Therefore, we have no need for the Director to attend this ruling. If you would plea so that we may move along."

"Not guilty," Alan snapped out of spite. "I don't understand half of the charges, so…"

A small screen rose up out of the floor, positioned at an angle so that the accused and the Board could view it. Footage began playing back from the bus accident.

"The accused registers a plea of not guilty," the Latina woman sighed, her short black hair forming around her face with a sharp line between her caramel skin. "Charge number one: reckless endangerment of the public. The accused is seen in vehicle surveillance tampering with the motor vehicle above, clearly causing disruption of the vehicle, the surrounding area, the second vehicle, and the passengers aboard said-vehicle."

"I was reacting to -," Alan tried to speak up. The woman looked up with unblinking, fiery eyes.

"The Board finds you guilty. The second charge: destruction of government property. As we can see in the playback, you clearly warp and manipulate government property, causing its full and ultimate destruction. The Board finds you guilty."

Alan decided he wouldn't speak up again. The dark-haired woman continued the sentencing.

"Charge number three: genetic perjury."

The charge amused Alan because it seemed like a strange way to talk about his ability. He also couldn't understand what they meant by perjury.

"Exhibit B of photographic evidence provided by satellite imagery, shows the crash scene in full detail. It clearly shows that the tree is pushed by its roots backward before the bus could make contact with it. This clearly demonstrates that the accused has lied under oath about his genetic deviation. He can not only manipulate magnetic fields, but, in fact, is capable of telekinetic episodes. We find the accused guilty of lying under oath under the Genetic Deviations Act."

Alan sat in wide-eyed confusion. It never occurred to him that he could move other objects. He always assumed that since he moved metal materials that he was a Magnet.

"Wait, I didn't know I -," Alan started, but was quickly rebuffed by the dark-haired woman.

"The fourth charge: insubordination. As our operator has disclosed, Alan Mitchell and Castor Baynes did not come cooperatively before this tribunal. Therefore, they have been found guilty.

"And the final charge: cross-contamination of a crime scene. As shown in Exhibit A and B, the accused knowingly exited the vehicle after the incident and interacted with the civilian's car, thus contaminating the crime scene as a known genetic deviation."

The military officer then spoke up, "This Board finds you guilty of all crimes as laid out by the Department for Mutated Persons investigation unit. Under section 28a of the Genetic Deviations Act, you are hereby taken into the complete and direct custody and care of the Board for such a time as is deemed necessary for full rehabilitation. Appeal is not granted. Dismissed for further questioning."

The Boar shut their files in unison, and the operator picked Alan back up at his shoulders and took him out of the room. Alan was dragged through a new hall with labels of B numbers and thrown into a concrete cell.

"You will be retrieved when we have further questions. Your abilities have very little use here, and we have 24/7 monitoring, so don't make me return."

Alan looked down at his cloth cot, and then caught something out of the corner of his eye. He stared at the wall across from him. Someone had scrawled in small, jagged letters.

"Hotel California."

nine

Hours. Days. Alan couldn't tell anymore. He was now clad in a white jumpsuit that had appeared during one of his short naps. When he changed into the jumpsuit, his street clothes disappeared during another subsequent nap. Alan could feel his personality ebbing away. Not a soul had come by since the operator had thrown him into his cell.

Alan spent most of his time attempting to train his so-called telekinetic abilities. The only thing he had to work with was his cot, so he spent hours on end trying to lift the cot while he sat up against a corner as far from it as he could.

Once he had successfully lifted the cot, he graduated to lifting the cot while he sat on top of it. That proved a little more difficult, but eventually he was able to raise the cot while sitting on it. Alan wobbled a little in the air, like a gymnast trying to stick the landing.

"Knock it off," a tinny voice echoed through a speaker in the hallway, cutting off Alan's concentration in the process.

The cot fell to the concrete floor, and Alan grumbled under his breath. A whooshing sound emanated from down the hall, and the operator walked up to Alan's cell. His eyes were half-open and his lips curled down in an annoyed frown.

"Get up."

Alan stood up reluctantly.

"Turn around."

Alan rolled his eyes and complied. The cell door slid open, and the operator stepped forward and gave Alan a pat down to check for any weapons or contraband. The operator then grabbed Alan by his shirt and pulled him back into the concrete hall. Alan looked at the drab, charcoal-colored concrete walls.

"We taking a stroll around the cell block?"

"Shut up," the operator replied, and he pushed Alan forward down the hall.

The operator took Alan into the D block, a long corridor filled with doors and mirrored, one-way glass. Once inside, Alan would no doubt be observed, unaware of the onlookers spying on him. The operator opened the door to D23, and then pulled Alan inside and sat him in an uncomfortable metal chair that screeched on the concrete floor when he landed.

"Wait here," the operator commanded, then he left through the door they had come from. Alan looked to his right. There was another pane of mirrored glass opposite the doorway they had come in. Alan felt like a rat in a maze. But was he going to get the cheese or the shock?

Directly across from Alan the wall opened, and a young man in a suit walked in.

"Mr. Mitchell," the man held out a hand across the table. Alan looked at it suspiciously, then gave the man a confused look. The man looked down at his own hand, and shook his head, "Excuse me, where are my manners? My name is Connor. I'm your legal representation."

Alan couldn't help but let out a thunderous laugh that echoed in the room. The lawyer seemed just as confused as Alan. Alan wiped the tears of laughter from his eyes.

"I'm sorry," Alan replied, then coughed. He continued, "Sorry. But you're doing a hell of a job, Connor."

Connor cleared his throat and set his briefcase down next to his seat, then he sat down across from Alan. They shared a brief moment of silence before Connor continued.

"I am here to help you mitigate your sentence through cooperation with the Board," Connor started.

"Yeah, that sounds more realistic. What do they want?"

Connor pulled out a folder from his bag and tossed it onto the table. Inside were several photos of Alan standing next to Marshall.

"The Board believes you have access to information about this individual."

"I know Marshall. Yes. That's about all the information I have," Alan replied. He knew it was partially a lie. Marshall had shared a lot with him that night after the bus accident. But he wasn't about to sell out his friend to help big brother get an advantage over him.

"We - ahem - the Board are aware that you are close with Marshall Roberts. Bearing that attempts to extract information from Mr. Roberts have been fruitless, and operatives have had little success as well, the Board has decided to offer you an incentive. If you can provide us with information on Mr. Roberts' associates, then the Board will consider your parole from this system."

"Associates?"

"We are aware that Marshall Roberts has divulged certain details and/or whereabouts of his family to you. This information is deemed an organization imperative by the Director of the Board."

"I'm not sure I know what you're talking about," Alan played dumb, folding his arms over his chest. The lawyer didn't respond to Alan's body language and continued his questioning.

"One of our informants is giving us live playback of your thoughts, Mr. Mitchell. Please don't play dumb with us," Connor retorted. Alan looked to the mirrored glass. No doubt, a reader was standing behind the glass. Alan considered how selfish a person could be to use their abilities against their own kind. Then he thought of how he harmed Molly. Connor held a hand to his ear, clearly taking in some bit of information.

"Mr. Mitchell, we would be willing to overlook your murder of Molly Dawes if you were to cooperate with the Board."

Alan could feel a burning in his chest and a lump in his throat. He felt violated. He looked over at the mirrored glass, his eyes watering and mouth drying up.

"Why don't you tell whoever's behind the glass that using my past against me isn't going to get them what they want," Alan looked back at Connor.

Alan could feel tears forming in his glossy eyes. Connor paused for a moment, clearly listening to the other side.

"Your guilt clearly says otherwise, Mr. Mitchell."

Alan slammed his fist on the table. The table - though bolted to the floor - shook angrily.

"I'm trying to help you," Connor replied calmly. The outburst clearly hadn't shaken him in the slightest. But it wasn't meant for him, but for the person behind the glass. Alan heard a switch flick and the hallway-side mirror turned transparent. Alan could see the operator on the other side shaking his head disapprovingly. "Another outburst, and we'll send you back to your bed."

Alan looked back to his right at the glass still opaque, its mirrored glass still hiding the Reader. He felt like a wounded animal. A wounded animal that was being kicked after the fact. Insult to injury.

Alan started to think deeply about his surroundings. The room, the lawyer, the operator, the mirrors, the informant Reader. He felt outside of himself. He looked down and saw the room from above. Outside of himself, he could float around and see what appeared invisible before. The taser strapped underneath the table next to Connor. There was a small switch panel next to the door he had entered. The operator's hand was on the mirror switch, about to flip back to the opaque function of the window. Alan's mind floated back to the other side, using his perception to find the other panel. He flipped the switch, and the mirror on his right side turned clear as day.

Alan looked into her eyes, the informant reader's squinting eyes. She didn't realize at first that Alan could see her. But then it became painfully obvious as his eyes locked with hers, like they were caught in the headlights of an oncoming car.

"*Athena?*"

ten

H ours passed. The interrogation was over, but Alan was still playing it back in his memory. How could Athena do this to the 308? They were friends; at least he thought they were friends. But it was becoming clear to him: she was the enemy. She was just like the rest of the traitors working for the Board.

"Alan," Athena stood in front of his thick glass cell door.

Alan didn't get up.

"Hello, *officer*," he replied with biting sarcasm.

Athena didn't reply for a while.

"I'm sorry about Molly."

"Clearly you are overwhelmed with sympathy," Alan snapped back.

Athena pulled a chair over to the glass wall and sat down in front of Alan. She was no longer in the custom work garb of the 308, but an operator's uniform. It was all black, with military style pockets on her long sleeve shirt and pants.

"Do you want to talk about it?" Athena asked, her tone soft and her speech rate slowing.

"Not with you," Alan replied and looked up at the camera over his cell, "Not with them."

Athena looked up at the camera. Several uncomfortable minutes passed, then Athena put her hands on her lap.

"My parents hated my gift," Athena started.

"Gee, I wonder why," Alan responded sarcastically.

"I deserve that."

"Damn right," Alan replied.

Athena cleared her throat, "My parents didn't understand at first. It seemed like I was really intuitive, perceptive. I would read their emotions before they even acknowledged them. I wouldn't come down for dinner because I knew they were mad at each other. Then I started using it against them. I'd play one off the other to get what I wanted. It ended up being very destructive to their relationship."

"Is this supposed to make me feel bad for you?" Alan questioned.

Athena continued, "Eventually I realized that I was better off being honest with them. I told them what I was doing. I tried to help their marriage. We talked things through, and that seemed to make things better for all of us. And then I stopped reading them. I tried to pretend I never read them at all. Life seemed normal for a while. Until I heard my dad thinking about Miss Katherine down the street."

Alan didn't say anything.

"I didn't tell my mom. How could I?" Athena recounted, "About a week later, I came home, and the house was really quiet. I wasn't sure if maybe they'd gone out for the afternoon. Until I walked into the kitchen."

Alan swallowed the scratchy rock lodged in his raw throat.

"My mom was bent over the kitchen sink washing her hands raw. Just scrubbing… scrubbing the layer of skin right off. There was blood all over the place… the sink… the tile… chairs. I didn't even acknowledge my mom. I followed the blood into the hallway. Then the bedroom. My dad was dead on the floor, shot right in the back. Katherine Waltz was still in bed. I can still remember the look on her face. She was in complete shock. All eyes. No color in her skin. Like a ghost of a person."

Alan locked eyes with Athena.

"I can't help but wonder if I told my mom when I found out... They probably wouldn't be married, but... I mean, how do you come back from that?"

"I don't know," Alan replied. However mad he was at Athena, he couldn't help but reply. "I don't know."

Athena clicked her tongue and sucked in a shallow, shaky breath.

"I told myself that I couldn't let my lies kill anyone else. I know Marshall wouldn't understand that. He always thinks he can find a win-win situation, but we don't have those anymore. I just want to keep us from losing everything, ya' know?"

Alan shrugged. He understood Athena. The pain of thinking you could have kept someone from dying and didn't was a burden he was accustomed to. But was it worth this?

"I don't want us to lose," Athena reiterated.

"Why don't you tell me what to do. How does this end well for me?"

"I don't know," Athena said, her voice a faint whisper. "But if you know something about Marshall, you need to tell me."

"I can't."

"Then I can't help you."

"I didn't ask you to," Alan replied as Athena stood up. She pushed the chair back to the concrete wall across from Alan's cell, and wiped some tears from her eyes. She exhaled and walked back down the hall.

Alan was alone again. Marshall and Athena had been two of his only friends at the 308. But they had their issues. Alan wanted to be positive like Marshall, but he couldn't ignore what he'd seen since joining the work camp. People had been imprisoned, beaten, and oppressed. It didn't sit right with him. Athena was more realistic about their situation, but she was also in the Board's pocket. She had sold out her friends to feel in control. Alan couldn't do that. He wouldn't. Alan decided he wasn't going to give Marshall up, no matter how bad it got in his cell.

~ ~ ~

Days passed. Alan hardly saw a soul, and he was left to fester in his own dark thoughts. Was this how they did it? Would he eventually just succumb to the darkness of isolation? He ate very little and talked even less. He was starting to wonder how he would end it, when Athena walked back up to his cell. Athena cleared her throat, trying to swallow the lump forming.

"Back again I see," Alan said, his voice scratchy and defeated.

"We don't get to decide what they'll do," Athena said. "We can only make our situation better."

It seemed to be a planned speech to Alan. Athena was firmly standing, no need for a chair.

"You certainly made yours better," Alan retorted under his breath. Athena sighed.

"Just give them what they want, Alan. It doesn't have to be this way."

"No?" Alan questioned sarcastically. "You mean I can go back home, with my judgmental parents and their awkward stares. Back to the town that remembers my dead girlfriend, and the freak who got her killed. I don't have anywhere to go back to."

107

"You could go back to the 308," Athena said, her voice a little less sure than before.

"We both know they would never let that happen, Athena. You seem to be the only one with privileges like that," Alan said in a low, angered voice. Alan continued, resigned to his sentence, "No, I'm stuck in here now, and the only thing I can do is make someone else's life worse by cooperating with you."

"You've been rehearsing this," Athena said in a somber tone.

"So, have you," Alan snapped back. "How long have you been spying on Marshall, hoping he would give you enough information to screw him over? Who does that to their friends? Sorry, that would imply you and Marshall are friends, and not his mark. What does that make you?"

Athena's face was like stone, her jaw tight and tense. She could tell she would fall apart soon if she couldn't get a grip on herself. She had to stick to the script.

"We don't have the luxury of having friends, Alan. They don't let us. Eventually everyone breaks and you do whatever the hell they want you to."

"No. Screw that," Alan pointed at Athena forcefully, "That's bullshit. We have a choice. We get to decide what to do with the time we have. You can trick yourself into believing whatever you want, but the truth is simple: We don't have to put up with this."

Athena scoffed at Alan's remark.

"We're both too realistic for you to believe that, Alan. We live on their terms."

Alan stood up from his cot and came to the thick glass right in front of Athena. She seemed uncomfortable by the change in demeanor.

"I wanted to be realistic - maybe even cynical - about this situation. I really did. You spend enough time talking to yourself in your head, you begin to think there's two of you. It's terrible to think you have a friend that's really just your subconscious kicking ideas back. But you've made me realize something, Athena. There's the prison cell you get thrown into, and there's the cell you put yourself in. I can tell you; I know which one is worse."

Alan looked in Athena's softening eyes. She wrapped her arms around her chest and looked at the concrete floor and her shifting black boots.

"It's over, Alan. We lost. They won."

"It's not that simple," Alan replied, "And deep down, you know that too. It might take a while to figure that out, but you will come to realize you're only as trapped as you make yourself."

"Funny coming from the man locked away," Athena rebuked Alan, her voice weak. Alan scoffed, and looked at the thick glass wall between them.

"You know, Marshall is naive. He thinks everything is great, and we just have to make the best of it. And there's you. You can see the 308 for what it is: a prison. But you also think that we're stuck following orders, and we're just whatever they want us to be. But that's not who we are."

"Then who are we?" Athena questioned in a patronizing tone, with her eyes still glued to the floor beneath her swaying legs.

"We're special."

Athena rolled her eyes.

"You're special," Alan continued. "We can do things people decades ago could barely imagine. We could build wonders. We live in a time of miracles. And we're squandering it allowing ourselves to be prisoners to people who don't understand and don't care about us."

"It doesn't matter that they don't understand or care, Alan. They're in charge," Athena pleaded for Alan to see reason.

"That may be, but the day will come when no manner of jail cell will hold us back, and nothing will stop us from seeing the light of day. We aren't meant to rot away. Humans... deviations... they're the same. We're the same, and we're meant to do something amazing."

Athena could feel tears welling up in her. Either Alan had grown desperate, or the solitude had cultivated something inside his soul that was bearing fruit.

"What you are implying is revolution," Athena said, her voice grave with fear.

"I'm not implying anything. I thought what I said was pretty straightforward," Alan smiled.

"They'll never let it happen, and they will get Marshall's information out of you," Athena said, now resigned to the fact that her friend was going to die before he gave up.

"I'm quite content to bide my time. Eventually, they're going to get bored with me. Then they'll get rid of me."

"What good is that?" Athena pleaded. "Alan, they'll kill you."

"It will be on my terms, and I won't bring Marshall down with me. We can't give up what brought us together."

eleven

A thena walked in the round room where the board had sentenced Alan two weeks prior. Alan was still not cooperating with her, and had, in fact, grown more zealous in his confinement. The Board was getting impatient, and they had called a meeting to discuss their options moving forward.

The Board member in glasses, a lanky black man from the Midwest, arrived early for the Board meeting and was trying to organize himself at the desk.

"Secretary Glasser," Athena said respectfully, nodding slightly. Glasser nodded back at her and carried on with his work.

The door opened again, and the military official entered with a briefcase in tow. Athena stood at attention.

"General."

"As you were," the General replied, and he sat down next to Glasser.

"Have you heard from the Director?" Glasser asked without looking up from his paperwork.

"We haven't spoken since he called for the meeting, no. Did you hear something?"

"No, no. Just wondering what this is about," Glasser replied.

The door opened and the other members of the board entered. First, the blonde woman, who was a judge in the Department for Mutated Persons. The second woman, who had short dark hair, was Deputy Director of the Board.

"Deputy Director Jimenez," Athena nodded. Jimenez ignored Athena and began addressing the rest of the Board.

"The Director asked me to begin, and he'll be here shortly. Where are we at with Alan Mitchell?" Deputy Director Jimenez asked.

The Board turned and looked at Athena. She cleared her throat and reported in.

"We still haven't been able to get information about Marshall Roberts. Mr. Mitchell has proven tougher to crack than previously expected."

"I say we start phase two, and crack this kid open like an egg," the General spoke up out of the group. "We don't have time to just wait for him to soften up on his own."

The Deputy Director spoke up, "Marshall Roberts' family must be found. Now, if you're willing to risk scrambling that idiot's brain to get your answers, and lose the only feasible lead we've had in years... Well, we'll let the Director know how you feel."

Everyone seemed wary when the Director was mentioned. Athena didn't know him, but from what she could tell, she didn't want to.

"Don't try to intimidate me, Miss Jimenez. I've seen far too much to be frightened by a little girl from Sedona," the General fired back, smacking his fist on the desk.

The Deputy Director didn't even acknowledge that the General had spoken. Instead, she was shuffling her papers and making notes with a ballpoint pen in the margins. Her silence gave the General pause. The General cleared his throat, looking at the other members of the Board.

The wall opened and an older man with graying hair and a dark, navy suit entered. The other members of the Board stood from the seats.

115

"Good afternoon, everyone," the man said, his light blue eyes shifting from one person to the other. The Deputy Director handed the man his folder with the day's notes. "Thank you, Sofía. You all can have a seat."

Everyone sat down, and the Director walked around to the front of the desk to face the rest of the Board.

"Mr. Director," the General spoke up, "I would like to start our proceedings today with the Marshall Roberts case."

"As far as I'm concerned, General, that's the only case," the Director replied, dropping his folder onto the desk. "I see from the notes that we're having some issues with Mr. Mitchell's interrogation."

"I have advised we move into Phase Two," the General chimed in.

The Director looked down at his folder, and then looked at the rest of the Board.

"And the rest of the Board members?" the Director asked. Glasser was leaning back in his chair, hand on his face with his thumb under his chin. His face seemed less than enthused.

"I'm not sure that would be prudent," Glasser advised.

"Our results with Phase Two have been inconclusive and dangerous," Deputy Director Jimenez reported, "I told the General as much before you arrived. I think we have to take our time."

"And I think we've waited long enough. It's great that Marshall came quietly, but his siblings are just as dangerous to this Department. We have to be willing to take the risk. I believe the reward outweighs the risks involved with Phase Two," the General implored.

"General," the Director interrupted aggressively – bordering on shouting at the General – but then his voice became calm once again. "We risk losing our only lead, and you want to use a dangerous, unfounded technique that could kill our lead or leave him in a vegetative state... because you're impatient?"

The General swallowed the lump in his throat.

"Now, I picked you for this Board because I thought you were level-headed, but my instincts have proven wrong it seems," the Director continued, his voice calm and menacing.

"I-I-I wasn't," the General stammered. The Director raised his head, his eyes looking down at the General at a condescending angle. "I merely think that the longer we wait the more dangerous it will become for this Department."

The Director hummed, his head returning to a more normal angle. He looked over at the Deputy Director, who had an unsure look on her face.

"Judge Hastings, what do you think?" the Director asked.

The judge sat up in her chair, her blonde hair wagging behind her. She took out her reader glasses and looked down at the file.

"I think that prudence should win the day," Judge Hastings replied, "But we also have an objective at risk, and our very existence hinges on our ability to find and neutralize Marshall Roberts' cabal."

"We've received countless intelligence reports that this group has made numerous attacks on our installations across the country," Secretary Glasser added. "While I agree that the General's plan is reckless, I do also believe our time is precious. The longer we wait, the more likely a high-priority target will be destroyed by these genetic-terrorists."

"Deputy Director?" the Director turned to his right-hand woman. She nodded.

"The General has his points, and the rest of the Board has made a clear argument. I think we need to be cautious with any action that might damage the asset," the Deputy Director explained.

The asset? Athena had remained silent, taking in the meeting with a sense of detached observation. But they were referring to her friend as an asset. He was a tool, a plaything for these people to accomplish whatever they wanted; to be discarded at the earliest possible sign of inconvenience. Alan was important to them, for now. But the minute he wasn't...

"...I would advise we give ourselves another round of interrogation, before looking to alternative methods such as Phase Two," Deputy Director Jimenez concluded.

The Director nodded, pacing back and forth as he took in his Board's ideas. He adjusted his navy suit and stepped back a few paces from the curved desk of the Board. A white podium jutted out from the floor, and the Director pulled the touch screen attached to the podium up to his face.

"I am willing to move forward with Phase Two, after another attempt to gain information from the asset, Alan Mitchell. We will have to use more *advanced* methods in our next interrogation. And if he continues to be a problem, we will begin Phase Two with a neural data mine. I will sign off on Phase Two when we return to assess the efficacy of the interrogation," the Director typed in his notes on the touch screen and signed the document with his index finger.

"As Director, this directive is legally binding under section 5 of the Genetic Deviations Act. Anyone who circumvents my authority, whether intentional or unintentional, will be subject to immediate incarceration under Department oversight. You are dismissed. Enjoy the rest of your day."

The Board stood from their seats, shook hands, and left the room to return to whatever their normal lives were. The Deputy Director remained behind to talk with the Director. The Director turned to Athena, his eyes disappointed and coldly discerning.

"I hope that this next interrogation goes far better than your previous record, Operative," the Director replied condescendingly. "We're only as effective as our records show. I hate having to answer these questions to the Deviation Operations Committee. Senators are about as forgiving as you'd expect. Carry on."

The Director turned to his deputy, "Ms. Jimenez, can you please brief me on our current installation management?"

The Deputy Director nodded, and she motioned for the Director to follow her out of the room. As they left, Athena could hear the muffled voices become blaring thoughts.

"Have you ever witnessed the neural data mine work?" the Director thought as he asked aloud to his deputy.

"Not that I can recall," Ms. Jimenez replied. Out of over one hundred test subjects, a majority were comatose. The rest were dead. Athena swallowed hard.

"A rather unfortunate setback," the Director replied, as they walked through the sliding door toward D block. His thoughts wandered to Marshall. He would stop at nothing until Marshall's entire family was locked up. Athena shook her head and turned away from them.

Athena walked back toward the B block of the compound, where she thought of Alan waiting for a day that would never come. Athena bit her lower lip, as the B block doors slid open. Now more than ever before, Athena felt completely out of control, and she was afraid there was no way to fix it.

twelve

Alan used his abilities to keep from slamming to the ground. He felt a boot press into his back and push him to the concrete floor.

"Don't do that. Don't fight it," the interrogator said gruffly, his boot pressing Alan's body into the concrete.

Alan looked out from the corner of his eye, taking stock of the blood beginning to stain the gray concrete. This didn't *feel* like an interrogation. And from the look on the operator's face, there must have been some enjoyment on his end. Alan groaned, feeling the flesh around his eyebrow pulse.

"That's going to bruise," Alan sighed.

"This isn't a joke, kid. You're on the wrong end of this thing," the interrogator said, his body drawing heavy breaths.

"Clearly," Alan replied, turning his face to see the man, whose shadow was clouding his vision.

The interrogator peeled Alan's body off the floor and stood him up. He pulled the overhanging light to Alan's face to survey the damage. Maybe a cut. Maybe stitches?

"Eh, you'll live."

"Thanks, doc," Alan replied jokingly.

The interrogator punched Alan in the gut in retaliation. Alan felt his stomach leap past his lungs and through his throat. Alan leaned into the interrogator's body, feeling his legs turn to jelly underneath him.

"What did I say about the jokes?"

"Only after a few drinks?"

Alan was shoved back in his rickety, wooden chair so hard that he could feel it quake under his weight. His face felt warm, blood clearly spread across from his wounds and blurring his vision.

"This can end if you'll just tell us what we need to know."

"Okay. Okay," Alan replied, his voice raspy from the all the violence. He raised his hands up, "Okay. Marshall Roberts. His family is hiding in a traveling circus. There a part of the trapeze artists. Tight-rope walking, death-defying leaps. The works. It's a beautiful thing."

The interrogator exhaled. Then he kicked the chair out from under Alan, sending Alan to the floor. Alan felt a boot smash into his side. He moaned as the interrogator flipped the switch on a small intercom panel.

"Yeah, we're done here. He's not talking."

~ ~ ~

Alan wondered what Molly would say seeing him in his current predicament. She was the optimist of the relationship. And while he had considered himself the cynic, the events of the past few weeks were now starting to nudge him in another direction. Without darkness, light would have no meaning, but darkness was just as invisible without light. The genetic deviations - as the Department called them - were living in dark times, that much could be seen. But there was a sliver of light beaming underneath the doorway. Alan wondered what was on the other side.

Alan hadn't seen Athena since their last conversation. He wasn't sure how much of what he said to her had been what she needed to hear or just desperate bargaining for her to see the light that Alan was starting to get glimpses of. Alan mused that it all bordered on insanity. He was in a no-win situation; a prisoner in a top-secret government installation. But as much as Athena wanted to persuade Alan that he was stuck, that his life was not his own, Alan felt a sense of freedom in his cell.

In solitude, Alan had found a new sense of himself. There was something in him that nothing on the outside world could hope to affect. He felt untouchable in his new center. And if he couldn't be touched, he didn't have to fall apart at the thought of prison or torture or death. There was a little light in the crack of the doorway, and that meant that darkness would never fully win. But it also meant something more than that. He had to keep the light from going out.

"I'm going to try one last time," Athena was standing in front of Alan's cell, a look of agonizing desperation in her face. She was overwhelmed with the option in front of her. "I'm running out of options here, Alan."

"I thought you were in control," Alan said sarcastically, not in a mean tone but levity.

"I thought I was too," Athena replied, exhausted. "Maybe you were right about me."

"That would be a first," Alan smiled, then raised his eyebrows and titled his head to the right. "I don't even know if I'm right about me."

"They told me this is my last try," Athena started again. "Then they'll start Phase Two."

"Oh? Phase Two," Alan joked, "Sounds terrifying."

"It is," Athena replied, her eyes on the concrete floor. "It is, and I don't want you to go through it, Alan. You can't."

"That's not really up to me, Athena," Alan remarked.

"It is," Athena pleaded, tears starting to well up in her eyes. "It is up to you. If you tell them what you know, they won't have to do it."

"Then they'll kill me, and they'll kill Marshall and everyone close to him. This is how you make people disappear. It's the easiest way. You don't incarcerate them forever. You don't re-assign them to another camp. When they've lost their value, you kill them. Once I give them what they want, I have nothing left to offer."

"Not nothing," Athena replied, pain written on her face.

"It's good to see they haven't completely bought you," Alan replied, his head resting up against the concrete wall next to his cot. "Maybe one day that will start something that ends this whole mess."

Alan lifted his hand. Athena's shirt collar pulled upward and wiped the tears from her eyes. Alan put his hand down, and the collar rolled back down.

"I'm not a martyr. I'm just tired of not caring, and this seems the only way to start," Alan explained. "You're not going to get any information out of me, Athena. I don't hold you responsible for what happens next, but I do hope you'll see now: you won't have control until you admit you don't."

Athena gave Alan a quizzical look, but it soon faded to sadness. Alan was accepting Phase Two.

"Fine."

Alan looked up and Athena was gone.

~ ~ ~

"Put this on," Athena said, as she threw a black uniform onto Alan's cot.

Alan cleared his throat.

"Oh, right," Athena replied, a red hue of blush forming around her cheeks.

Athena turned away while Alan took off his prison garb and slipped on the black uniform.

"So: Phase Two?" Alan asked. Athena nodded solemnly.

"We can still stop this, Alan. You don't have to go through with it if you just cooperate with them," Athena pleaded as she took Alan out of the cell.

"I can't, Athena," Alan said.

Athena's hands shook as the carbon-fiber shackles were locked to Alan's hands. He looked into her eyes and saw her anguish. Athena couldn't handle the eye contact and looked away. She put a hand on Alan's shoulder and led him down the hall.

Athena's skin felt flush as they got closer to C block, the experimental wing of the installation. At first, her heart was racing as her anxiety grew. But there came a tipping point, where she felt her emotions fall over the side of a wall; from anxiety to anger. How dare they make her choose this path?

Athena felt the remote in her pocket pulsing. Alan's words were echoing in her brain. The first step to taking back control was admitting you were out of control. They stood at a three-pronged juncture in the hallway. Forward would take them to the interrogation rooms Alan had been in before. On the right was the hallway that led to the exit. And the left. The left would take them to the experimental wing.

Athena cleared her throat and pushed the button on the remote. The fluorescent lights overhead shut down, leaving a trim of red lights on the ground to barely illuminate the few inches in front of their faces. Alan felt himself pushed to his right, into a side room. He could barely see Athena's outline, but he could hear her frantic breathing.

"Listen, we don't have much time. I'm getting you out of here before the normals scramble your brain, okay?" Athena said quickly, as if the answer wasn't insane and suicidal.

"This is crazy, you know that, right?" Alan replied. Athena regained some sense of vision in the little closet they had rushed into. She pulled bits of cloth off of Alan's black uniform revealing an Operator's disguise.

"This is crazy."

"Yeah, you keep saying that," Athena said, her voice a little annoyed. "Did you think I was going to let them scramble you?"

"I didn't know what to think," Alan said.

Athena shoved a tactical helmet on Alan's head. She tapped it playfully, then pulled Alan close to her face.

"Don't make me regret this, Alan."

"We need to get Castor and Nick," Alan replied.

Athena shook her head, "Are you crazy? I didn't bust you out so you could go back to the detention block. There's no way. Just take this hall down to the exit, tell them your number, and they'll send you wherever you want to go. Just get as far away from here as possible. Run and hide. Don't let them find you, okay? I'm going to be really pissed off if I hear they caught you."

Alan smiled.

"I can't leave you. I can't leave them. I can't leave Marshall."

"Oh my god, I'm starting to hate this self-righteous, martyr bullshit. Just let me save you. Go have a long and uneventful life somewhere in the boonies and forget all this crap we've been through. Don't waste this."

"You know I can't."

Athena rolled her eyes, pulled Alan to her lips and kissed him like they'd never meet again. Athena pushed him back, Alan's eyes wide in confused wonder.

"If you tell Marshall I kissed you, I'll kill you myself."

Alan stumbled out of the closet and walked as fast as he could down the hall. Athena walked out of the closet, the light still dim, as the system started coming back online. Alan looked back at her. Athena shook her head no. She wasn't coming along for the ride.

"I can't," she mouthed, and she turned away toward the C block hall.

Alan realized the minute the lights came back on in his hallway, the cameras would be back on him. The disguise wouldn't last forever. He walked as swiftly as possible without feeling conspicuous. The wall opened to reveal another circular room with an Operator standing in the center.

"Where to -?"

"Number 227," Alan replied to her. "I'm reporting to precinct 308."

The woman nodded and held her hand out between them. A blue pool opened, and Alan stepped through.

Pulled apart, scrunched together, then spit out onto the cool, wet grass of the 308's courtyard. He'd never get the hang of teleportation. The pool closed up in a flash of blue light, the air swirling around him in a small vortex. A cold fog remained like a blanket around him.

"What in the hell is going on out here?" Alan heard Finch's voice call out from the lobby.

The fog cleared and Finch found himself looking down at Alan, both them looking at each other with terrified stares.

"Well, this isn't good."

thirteen

"What did you do, little girl?" the Director's voice punctuated every word with disdain.

Athena felt the cuffs strangling her hands behind her back, tension pulling them downward with an Operator's hands pressing down on them with force. Athena winced, the metal chafing the skin raw. A small part of her was regretting helping Alan. But only a small part. She did remember the kiss now. It was impetuous, but the time seemed to call for it. Now she was wondering what it would all mean if she could make it out of her situation alive. But that was unlikely.

"You know what I did," Athena grunted, as the Operator pulled back on her cuffs. She could feel her wrists burning as the cuffs raked her with every pull.

The Director put his right hand over his temple, fighting off the migraine forming around his skull like a pulsing net. He ran his tongue across his top teeth, then along his bottom lip. He nearly snarled at the stupid girl.

"We don't have time for this," the Director groaned. "I'm sure the young man has gone to Marshall Roberts already."

"I told him to run and hide," Athena interjected.

The Director rolled his eyes and looked at Athena with annoyance dripping from his gaze.

"Forgive me if I don't believe you. Regardless, why would he listen to *you*. Take her to C block for neural data mining. Send a team to the 308. We're going to fix this, *now*."

The operator yanked Athena down the hall. Deputy Director Jimenez jogged up to the Director, electronic tablet in hand.

"What is it?" the Director said through pregnant pauses. Jimenez pursed her lips, annoyed. She looked down at her tablet.

"We have a situation. The escape has caused a panic in the capital."

"Now, how would they know about that?" the Director questioned.

"If I were to guess: the General."

"Of course," the Director muttered. "Well, you know what to do about him. I don't have time to deal with this bullshit. Get a teleporter agent ready, and we'll talk with those sniveling senators."

~ ~ ~

"I don't have time to explain," Alan replied to Finch, who seemed to be on the verge of a panic attack. It was lights out, so no one else was in the courtyard, but it wouldn't take long if they kept talking like they were. "They'll be coming for me."

"Are you kidding me? You brought them *here?*" Finch asked, feeling a twitch in his eye. He slid an uneasy hand down his face. These kids were going to give him a stroke. Finch picked Alan up by the arm and pulled him into one of the rooms, Marshall's room.

"Kid?" Marshall was groggy and shocked. Finch pushed Alan into Marshall's bulky chest and shut the door behind them.

"Mr. Mitchell here is bringing the Department to the 308, so you're going to hide him."

"What are you going to do?" Alan asked as he peeled himself off of Marshall.

"This is your problem kid. I'm not the one who got us in this mess."

135

"That's not fair, Finch," Marshall replied.

Finch rolled his eyes. "None of this is fair, Roberts. It's all a shitshow, but we deal with the punches as they come. And I'm going to deal with this so our whole precinct doesn't get wiped, okay?"

Marshall had no response. Neither did Alan, save for a conflicted look on his face and a pounding heart. He was starting to second guess himself. Everything seemed to point to returning to get Marshall, but now he was afraid the rest of the people at the 308 were in jeopardy because of his actions. Finch left Marshall's room in a violent huff. Marshall opened his dresser drawer and pulled out some of Alan's things.

"They usually just toss people's stuff when they disappear. I grabbed some of your things."

Alan looked down at his broken watch. He strapped it to his wrist carefully.

"What happened to you, kid?"

"They're looking for your family, Marshall. Whatever deal you cut... it seems they don't care anymore. They knew you wouldn't give up your family, so they went after me," Alan answered. He could feel the sweat starting to build on his body. Now that he

136

was out, his adrenaline was just pushing him past the point of exhaustion. "The-they tried to get answers. They were going to even try to crack open my brain. But Athena…"

"Athena?" Marshall stopped Alan dead in his tracks. "What do you mean Athena?"

Alan hadn't considered how to broach the subject, but now, in his panic, he was confused about how to go forward about Athena.

"She was working for them, Marshall, but she isn't anymore. Or she is, but she helped me escape. I'm not sure. Either way, I'm scared they figured it out, and she won't be working with them for long. We have to break her out. Her and Castor and Nick and all the others locked up at the Department."

"She was working for the Department this whole time?" Marshall questioned. The punches just kept on coming. "No, screw her. She made her choice; we should get out of here."

"We can't leave them," Alan protested. His body felt cold and his skin felt white hot. His stomach was churning. He felt his blood pulsing through his body. He could feel the hairs standing at attention on his forearms. It was anxiety or obstinance. He couldn't tell if it was either or both, but he wasn't going to let this stand.

"They all made their choice, Alan. Like you and Athena always said, this is the world we live in. The best we can do is run while we still can," Marshall seemed detached from.

"*Run?*" Alan said, his eyes full of righteous anger. "I could've left you, man! I could've gone anywhere, and I came back to warn you. What the hell is your problem?"

"You don't understand these people, Alan. They'll take everything you have and then take some more!" Marshall was now yelling, "I left my whole family to save them, and now you want me to just throw that all away for your crusade? Screw that, kid. Screw that and the horse you rode in on."

Alan could feel tears in his face, because it was the only warm thing throughout his body.

"You're a coward."

"And you're a naive little boy with delusions of grandeur," Marshall raged. "Death makes cowards. Soldiers hate war. And the ignorant complain about their ideals while people get murdered in the street for being *other*. Just shut up and do what I say."

Alan clenched his jaw. He was about to start the argument again when he heard the distinct rushing sound of a portal opening in the courtyard.

~ ~ ~

Two operators basked in the blue glow of the portal, ominously standing over the courtyard with detached judgment.

"Agent Finch," one of the Operators shouted, "Your presence is requested."

Finch was sweating in the lobby when the portal had opened but found himself shaking in the doorway of the courtyard in the wake of the Operator's words. Finch reluctantly walked onto the courtyard turf.

"Can I help you, gentlemen?"

"We have reason to believe that Alan Mitchell - who has gone AWOL - fled to this location. We ask that you turn him over now."

"Hate to tell you guys, but he ain't here."

The Operator turned and addressed Finch with a condescending stare, towering a full foot over the older caretaker.

"Choose your words very carefully, Mr. Finch," the other Operator, a lanky man with blonde hair, replied.

"You've got a lot of nerve, kid," Finch replied, his teeth gritting together. "Why don't you scurry back to your keepers and let me run my precinct. I don't have time for this crap."

Finch felt his body seize up. One operator held his hand out, taking control of Finch's body. Finch felt gravity pull his knees to the ground. He looked up at the tall operator, whose hand was now reaching out and pressing down on him.

Alan looked through a slit in Marshall's window at the courtyard. He recognized the blond operator, the healer EMT from the bus accident. Linus.

"I have to go help."

Marshall grabbed Alan before he could reach the door.

"Let Finch handle this, Alan," Marshall replied.

Several people were starting to leave their rooms, driven by curiosity at the noise in the courtyard. Some of them were standing, mouths agape in shock at their caretaker on his knees.

"Go back to your rooms," the telekinetic Operator shouted to the gathering crowd. The crowd didn't move.

"Where is he?" Linus hissed through a clenched jaw at Finch.

"He's not here. And screw you," Finch sneered, his eyes looking up from inside his immovable head.

The telekinetic operator made a fist, and Finch groaned in pain.

"Do it," the telekinetic operator ordered to Linus. Linus held out his hand over Finch's heart. Finch could feel his heart pulsing rapidly. His mouth filled with a rusty flavor of blood. The heart pulsed faster. Faster. Faster. Pop. Finch's body fell limp down onto the courtyard ground.

The telekinetic operator turned to the stunned crowd.

"Where is Alan Mitchell?" the telekinetic operator shouted, his voice echoing in the courtyard.

The crowd changed from shocked to obstinate, their faces emotionless like stone.

"They're going to kill them," Alan growled at Marshall. "You don't understand, Marshall. These people don't care. They just have the mission."

Marshall shook his head no.

Linus whispered something into his earpiece, and a blue portal opened in the courtyard. A teleportation operator walked through with a dark-skinned man in plain clothes.

"Everyone," the man shouted. "I am your new supervisor, Mr. Torrence. We are looking for Alan Mitchell. Anyone with information to his whereabouts will be rewarded. If you do not comply with this department, your precinct will be liquidated. You have one hour to comply."

Alan turned and gave Marshall a furious look. "See?"

Marshall looked down at the crowd beginning to disperse. Finch's body remained limp on the ground amid the Department Operators, who were talking quietly to each other, likely about the crowd. Marshall watched the Department employees walk away into the lobby, leaving Finch's body on the ground.

"They aren't even going to bury him. But he's a normal. What the hell is going on?" Marshall grumbled under his breath.

"They. don't. care," Alan said slowly, each word a hammer strike on Marshall's ears. "Marshall, we can't keep living like this. Your family wouldn't want this for any of us."

"Don't pretend like you know anything about me, kid. I've lived long enough to know what lies at the end of this road, and it ain't pretty."

Alan exhaled in exasperation. He sat on the bed. He looked at Marshall. Then he remembered something.

142

"My mother used to tell me this story when I was younger. It was about these two friends."

Marshall rolled his eyes.

"These two friends lived in a small village in China. One was blind, had been blind for a long time. His friend, he lost his arms as a kid. Some genetic disease, I think. My mother told me that they would journey out into the countryside around their village. You want to know what these two supposed freaks did, Marshall?"

Marshall's body slouched. "What?"

"They went out to plant trees. Every day, they would get up and leave their homes. The man without arms would carry the blind man. The blind man would handle the seeds with the help of his friend. They would plant trees. Trees they would probably never see. I'm not sure why my mom told me that story. I think she wanted me to think it was okay that I was a 'freak'. But I think it means more than that."

"Kid," Marshall objected.

"But I get it now. Those people were going to get their trees - a better life - because those two friends didn't let the world get to them. They were going to make it something better than when they found it. And we could do that. But not if we just sit here and do our time. If we let them beat us down…"

Marshall was silent. It felt like hours to Alan. Marshall finally pointed to his bathroom.

"My bathroom has a window unit. You can push it out and escape. I'll make sure they never know you were here."

~ ~ ~

"Okay, we're going to cut to the chase," Linus whispered to his other operator, then he shouted at the crowd, "Where is Marshall Roberts?"

A chair flew out from the balcony level of the apartment complex, smacked Linus in the face and then bounced across the courtyard into a concrete beam holding the balcony up, cracking it in the process.

The telekinetic operator lifted his hand up, just as Marshall leaped from the balcony toward him. Marshall slowed in the air, until, finally, he was floating overhead.

"Insubordination and terrorist activities. Automatic three strikes," the telekinetic operator said with a smile, as he subtly spun

Marshall in the air. The teleportation operator opened the portal for exfiltration and stared back at the floating Marshall.

"Where is Alan Mitchell?" the telekinetic operator asked with curiosity in his voice. "Surely, he must be here."

"M-maybe you scared him off," Marshall grunted, his muscles spasming out of control. "You did put on ... quite a ... show."

Linus pulled himself up and whipped the dust and concrete pieces from his clothing. He fixed his broken arm with a warming hand, and pointed at his eyes, then at Marshall in an act of intimidation.

"Look... the kid's... gone. Okay? He knew you were coming. You were pretty... obvious," Marshall managed to get out. "I gave him the out... and... he t-took it."

The telekinetic operator's curiosity was gone. "We'll deal with him later. Your amnesty is up, Roberts. You're coming with us."

He pulled Marshall down to the ground, and the operators walked through the portal, leaving the rest of the 308 with their new supervisor, Mr. Torrence, and the teleportation operator.

Marshall felt himself pulled apart and pushed back together again as he was teleported into the circular entrance room of the

Department. The telekinetic operator came through with his partner and saw that something was amiss.

"What the hell?" the telekinetic operator sighed under his breath, his eyes meeting Alan Mitchell's.

"Hello," Alan said with a smirk, and he clapped his hands together, knocking the two operator's heads together with his telekinesis.

"Get up, Marshall. We've got work to do."

fourteen

Alan bent over the two operators' unconscious bodies, pulling their walkie talkies off their utility belts and unhooked them from their ear pieces. He tossed one to Marshall, who caught it.

"I almost thought you weren't going to come," Marshall admitted.

Alan chuckled, unbuttoning Linus's shirt, and tossing it to Marshall.

"I hope this fits," Alan joked.

"It's… snug," Marshall groaned, as the buttons felt like they might pop off. The pants were the same story; the same length, but the width was a little constrictive. Marshall looked down at the walkie talkie in his hand.

"What channel are we on?"

"Eleven," Alan replied, finishing up with his clothes. "I think their security is always on seven."

"You know, you didn't mention you could move things with your mind. I thought you were a magnet?"

Alan looked up, "I didn't know I could either. That was part of my sentence. They thought I was lying."

Marshall shrugged, "What's next?"

"I noticed teleportation messes with the magnetic fields. That's why they never put cameras in here. Would've just shorted them out every time. But the rest of the place has eyes and ears. We'll sneak around better in these uniforms. You're going to A block to break Castor and Nick out. It'll be a left fork in the road once we get out of here. I'll go to B block to find Athena. We'll try to meet up at the exit and get a teleporter to get us out of here."

"Okay," Marshall nodded.

"Give me a hand here," Alan said, and they pulled the two operators to the side of the central room, away from the doorway. Marshall clapped his hands together, as if dust had collected from the work. Alan chuckled a little and pointed at the almost seamless wall off to their right.

"The door's right there. Are you ready?"

Marshall nodded, adjusting his new, tight uniform.

"I feel dirty in this thing, but, yeah, I'm ready."

Alan walked up to the wall and the doorway split open with a soft whooshing noise. The metallic hallway seemed so much longer now that Alan wasn't being dragged through it by the guards. Alan swallowed the lump in his throat and led Marshall on their first steps down the hall. Alan could hear every boot step clang on the metal-grated floors, the sound rattling hollow in his ears. Alan cleared his throat as they reached the A block fork.

"Well, this is you," Alan said. Marshall nodded.

"Good luck, kid."

Alan watched Marshall turn the corner and begin the long walk down the A block corridor. Alan was finally aware he might be looking at his friend for the last time, a sinking weight in his gut. He shook off the feeling, exhaled a deep breath, and continued his long trek to the B block.

The hallway felt a lot longer without Marshall standing next to Alan. The hallway was lonely, and Alan was left with his thoughts. Athena. Castor. Nick. They were all casualties of a war that Alan couldn't quite understand yet. Alan didn't really know how things had gotten so bad for people like him. The events of the past few years had been a blur, with announcements from the federal news flashing warning signs here and there. But really, Alan had been absent-minded and content in his relationship with Molly. Like a satellite, Alan had orbited Molly. Now, he was in retrograde, burning up in the atmosphere. And it felt exhilarating.

During his time in B block, Alan knew that most of the guards took the maintenance hall, which ran a full circle around the central hub where the Department met. It was a way for guards and other workers to get around without having to interrupt meetings or get locked out of their blocks during Department meetings. Alan was going to use it to find a shortcut from the hub to B block, and, hopefully, find Athena.

Alan swiped his badge across the maintenance hatch, and the doorway slid open. The hall was an endless curve. It was a little disorienting at first, but Alan found his footing staring at the floor. It didn't take long to reach the hatch leading into the B block hallway.

Alan's boots, which were a tad loose for his taste, clanged onto the B block metal floor and echoed down the hall. The cells were filled with different people. But no Athena. Alan walked back down the hall and found one of the first inmates.

"Where's the girl?"

"The traitor?" the man asked smugly, with a deep chuckle in his throat.

"Yeah. The traitor," Alan said, his voice clearly annoyed.

"Man, I don't know where she went, but I know where she ain't," the inmate waved his hands around. He stood up from his cot and looked Alan in the eye. "Wait, a minute."

"Tell me where she went, and I'll bust you out of here," Alan said, his voice stern with purpose. The lights strobed and finally died, bathing the hall in a red hue. It reminded Alan of Athena and his previous escape. Marshall must've started commotion in A block.

The inmate gave a skeptical glance at the lighting, then at Alan. He cleared his throat and pressed his face to the thick, bulletproof glass. The inmate shook his head, finally making his decision.

"They took her to C block, man. I don't think you got a chance; but if you make it, I'll be right here."

Alan nodded, and ran off to find Athena in C block.

~ ~ ~

Marshall sent an A block guard into the metal wall across from the cells, knocking him out cold. Marshall grimaced as the guard thudded the metal surface and smacked the ground with a loud clang.

Another guard pulled his assault rifle and watched the bullets rip through Marshall's uniform, then they glanced off Marshall's impervious skin. Marshall's strength ran all the way down to the marrow, a miraculous feat shared by most strength-based mutations. Marshall grabbed the rifle out of the guard's hands and smashed the metal down like it was wet clay, letting the pieces rattle as they fell on the metal floor.

Marshall grabbed the guard and gently knocked him on the helmet, causing the guard to pass out instantly. It took a lot of practice to be careful with his abilities, but now it was second nature. The guard fell over, revealing Castor in Marshall's line of sight.

"Marshall? Damn, it's good to see you," Castor shouted from his cell. "I told Nick you guys would come back for us."

"Where is Nick?" Marshall looked around.

"They re-assigned him to a foundry, smelting or some nonsense. Sounded like bullshit to me. Where's the kid?"

"He's looking for Athena," Marshall said.

"Athena's here too? What a reunion we got going. The control panel's over there, boss."

Marshall walked over to the guard post, which had a large electrical panel, a metal desk with a computer and a stack of paperwork sitting on it.

"Just flip the switch, and I can get us out of here," Castor assured Marshall. Marshall nodded, and grabbed the switch on the electrical panel, just as another guard came in.

Unfortunately, the guard was strong like Marshall. He grabbed Marshall by the arm and flung him into the A block doorway. Marshall's body ached as he peeled himself off the metal wall, leaving a Marshall-sized dent in it. But as soon as he pulled himself off, the guard shoved Marshall right back into the wall.

"Stand down!" the guard shouted as he slammed Marshall's head into the wall again. And again. Marshall could feel his head was starting to get warm, blood definitely trickling down the side of his face. "Stand down - gah!"

Castor's red-hot hand grabbed the guard's right shoulder and pulled him off Marshall, who then slid onto the floor. The guard turned into the momentum and shoved Castor to the ground.

"Get back in your cell, now!"

"Screw you," Castor groaned, as he tried picking himself up. The guard shoved Castor again, this time sending him into the back wall near the guard post. Castor winced as his left arm - still aflame - melted through the wall near the electrical panel. Castor tried to bring his arm back out of the wall, but could feel it catch on the metal, so he gave up.

"That's what I thought," the guard taunted, as he stood over Castor's body.

"Yeah, yeah. Big tough guy," Castor joked.

"Ahem," Marshall cleared his throat, and the guard turned around to a haymaker to the face. Total Knock Out. Marshall picked the guard up and - using his eye beams - welded the guard's outline to the wall.

"I'd clap, but - ya know," Castor nodded to his arm tangled in the metal, "You seem to have found your calling, boss."

"Shut up," Marshall joked, and ripped the metal away around Castor's arm. "That better, you big baby?"

Castor rolled his eyes and pulled his bleeding arm out of the giant hole in the wall. Castor looked at the electrical panel then the hole.

"I have an idea."

"I'm listening," Marshall replied.

Castor's hands glowed white-hot. He followed the electrical panel wiring back into the hole. Castor concentrated, the heat traveling down the wires through the wall, and out of the room. Marshall could see the line of heat glowing as it traveled around the room where the electrical wire was placed.

"What're you doing?"

"Sending a shock to the electrical grid," Castor replied through clenched teeth. He pushed even further, and the wire started melting around his hand. The metal wall started to warp, bowing under the extreme heat. Lights began to strobe, then died, bathing the pair in a red light. "That should buy us a little more time."

~ ~ ~

Guards in tactical gear passed Alan as they ran toward the source of all the commotion. The light was still dimly red, and Alan used the panic to sneak his way into C block's usually secure gateway. Alan could tell its construction was a large circular room like the hub, but it was made up of small labs stitched together with a honeycomb of hallways. And like the hub, C block had a circular hall running along the outside of the block.

Unlike the rest of the wings, C block was bathed in sickly fluorescent light; still powered by a separate backup generator.

Alan looked back through the doorway and saw that B block was still blood-red. He wondered if C block ran on its own power source for a reason. Alan shrugged, and made his way down the central hall that bisected the circular complex. He stood at the intersection and saw that the detention area was down to the right. But Alan's gut told him the large 'Special Projects' sign on his left would be where Athena was being held for the neural data mine.

fifteen

Alan stood quietly in the lab room; his eyes set ahead at the woman unconscious on the table. She looked ironically peaceful given the surroundings. The heart monitor beeped steadily in the corner, while an IV pumped fluids and sedative through the woman's veins. They were running out of time; the guards wouldn't be distracted forever.

Alan gently pulled the IV from the woman's arm and waited for her to wake up. He could hear men running down the halls and shouting to one another. Then there were men at the door, slamming viciously at the metal work. Alan had destroyed the lock mechanism, so it would take at least two more minutes before they could get the door down. Or not.

The door exploded open, debris flying inside the white room, rattling off walls and shredding the medical equipment like it was tissue paper. Alan protected the woman, curving the explosion of metal all around them and onto the back wall.

"Hands on your head!" the voices shouted in near unison. Alan turned his head to the side to see flashlights and assault rifles fixed to them, shining back at him. He could probably stop most of their bullets. Most, not all; and he wasn't feeling especially bleedy at the moment. He put his hands over his head, and the men ran forward.

"On the ground!" the voices shouted in panicked bursts of air. Two men pushed Alan to his knees, while others swarmed the woman lying on the table.

"Get the IV back in! Put it back!" one yelled to another, but it was too late.

The black-haired woman's eyes opened, and she screamed bloody murder. Alan looked up at the ceiling and watched as it began pressing down towards them. The back wall folded in on itself, revealing a dark abyss. The floor beneath the soldiers began to shift like a moving escalator, causing the men to fall over. Alan could feel vertigo setting in, his mind overtaken with dizzying nausea. The floor slowly tilted upward, causing soldiers to roll towards the side walls. Alan reached out to keep himself centered on the floor. He watched as one soldier slipped into the side wall, screaming as he fell, stuck inside of it like a two-dimensional piece of paper.

Another soldier grabbed the IV stand as it slid, trying to use it to push himself away from the wall that was swallowing his comrades. The IV stand swung wildly, snapping the soldier's arm at the elbow like a chicken wing. Alan shut his eyes in sheer terror at the sight.

"Don't be afraid," the woman's voice cut through the chaos of the situation, as if it was inside Alan's head rather than an audible sound.

Alan felt a cold hand wrap around his, so he opened his eyes. The woman was kneeling down beside him, a look of whimsical curiosity set on her brow. Alan looked around. The soldiers were all writhing around on the floor, panicked breaths and grunts swelling in their chests.

"What the he-?" Alan's voice trailed off, his confusion more like bewildered madness than genuine curiosity.

"They'll be fine," the woman assured, and she helped Alan to his feet.

The room no longer felt like it was spinning; at least, for him the room had returned to normal. The men continued in their frenzied panic, unaware they were living in a prison of their own imaginations.

"You seem confused."

"I thought you were…" Alan breathed fully for the first time since entering the room.

"You were expecting her," the woman replied, filling in Alan's gaps. "I'm sorry I'm not."

The woman looked up, her face suddenly aware of an urgency.

"Come with me," the woman spoke calmly, pulling Alan with her out the doorway and into the white-tiled hallway. Alan saw a great deal more soldiers rolling around in the halls as they went.

"They think they're on fire," the woman said plainly, her voice soft and lacking any emotional fluster. "Alright, let's go."

"We aren't going anywhere. Not until we find her," Alan pleaded with the mysterious woman, his hands shaking from the adrenaline rush.

The woman opened the metal double doors in front of her and motioned for Alan to leave. Alan moved his hand back, and the doors snapped shut. The woman looked back, partly impressed and partly annoyed.

Alan's eyes narrowed. He straightened his uniform and pointed back the way they had come.

"I said no. Athena is in here, and I'm not going to leave her because you're scared of the boogeyman."

"Scared? You're damn right, I'm scared. Did you see what they did to me in there?" the woman questioned, her tone shrill and upset. "I'm not going back."

"You won't have to, but we have to find my friend - and now - before they scramble her brains," Alan said firmly. "You have my word; I won't let them hook you back up to that machine."

The woman composed herself, then nodded in agreement. "She's probably in the neural data mine. It's over there."

The woman pointed to the hallway heading to the detention area. Alan rolled his eyes. Of course.

"How do you know that's where it is? You've been unconscious."

"I can read minds, dummy. Just as easy to pull information as it is to put in."

"Fair enough."

Alan shrugged. If Athena could read minds, and this woman could make people see things, he supposed that there was an overlap somewhere in there to do both. It wasn't in him to protest the gifting of other freaks. He thought he could only move metal, and now he was moving anything he felt like... with his mind. Best not to question a fellow freak.

"Good point, -," Alan held his hand out, waiting for her to finish with her name.

"Elizabeth," the woman held out her hand.

"Nice to meet you, Elizabeth. Alan," Alan replied and pointed to the hall awkwardly, "To the brain thingy."

~ ~ ~

Athena looked up at the circular dish standing over her head.

"Please, try to relax, ma'am. Struggling will only make it worse," the doctor said calmly at Athena's bedside.

"Yeah, sure. I'll relax just fine... once you unplug me, Dr. Frankenstein."

Athena tensed up, more to spite the amicable mad scientist. The doctor cleared his throat and placed electrodes around Athena's temples. The doctor pulled some switches, and Athena could hear a faint ringing sound in her ears.

The doctor typed a few deliberate keystrokes into his computer, and the machine over Athena's head began to light up and beep.

162

Athena closed her eyes, as the machine spun, emitting a sound like a loud vacuum cleaner. Then shattering, metal crashing, and the doctor screaming. Athena could feel her restraints lifting. She opened her eyes.

"Hey," Alan said, his voice soft. Athena could feel a smile overtaking her face. It was automatic. She couldn't tell if it was about the rescue or that she saw Alan's friendly face again.

"You idiot. I told you to run."

"I mean, I could hook you back up if you'd like," Alan teased, then brushed the hair out of her face. "Let's just get you up, and you can yell at me some more later."

Their moment was broken up by the blood-curdling screams of the scientist, whose arms were spastically pawing at the floor. Both Alan and Athena jumped at his first panicked cry. Alan felt the hairs on his arms stand. Athena, the same. The scientist's glasses had cracked at the bridge of his nose, as his face desperately pressed against the concrete floor, trying to escape some illusion.

"I'm going to drown!" the doctor shrieked. "Save me! Someone help!"

"How?" Athena looked around. "Should we do something? Who did this to him?"

Elizabeth walked into her line of sight. Athena gave her a confused look. Elizabeth put a hand to her chest.

"Elizabeth," she replied to Athena.

Athena groaned, as her shackles came off. Alan pulled her up, embracing her tightly.

"I hate to rain on the parade, but it's time to get out of here," Elizabeth said in a dry tone. "Let's go."

~ ~ ~

Marshall barreled his way through the crowd of guards standing in the circular hallway near the hub, pushing them off as he ran. Castor ran behind him, punching with fire-laced fists and melting firearms in his burning grip.

Marshall and Castor were about to be overwhelmed from both sides when the C Block hallway door blew open, slamming guards into the ringed hallway's metal siding. Alan came walking through.

"Nice trick," Castor said, exhaling and hunched over. He wasn't used to so much cardio.

"Follow me," Alan said, "Let's get to the exit. I have some more friends coming, but we can pave the way."

Alan slammed his way through a group of guards and into the exit door, startling a teleportation operator on the inside. The Asian woman's eyes were terrified when she realized what was happening. But it was too late. She lifted her hands up to initiate a portal, but Alan raised one hand out, and she became stuck like a statue.

Marshall grabbed her, holding his hand around her mouth.

"Listen, don't scream, ok. We're not going to hurt you," Marshall said in a calming tone. The woman nodded. Marshall let her go, and she tried to punch him. Marshall grabbed her arm like she was a child. "I told you we wouldn't hurt you. I forgot to mention: don't hurt us."

The woman struggled for a minute, writhing around, trying to get a holding that would give her leverage. Marshall looked up at

Castor, who was trying to fight laughter. Marshall rolled his eyes and lifted the woman over his head.

"I can do this all day. *All. Day.*"

She took the hint and gave up.

"What do you want?" the woman said through an annoyed groan.

"We want out of here, lady," Castor replied sharply. "What the hell kind of question is that? You ever hear a prisoner say, 'Oh, come to think of it. I was going to break out, but - nah - just give me some steak and we're square.' Jeez, these people, right?"

The woman gave Castor an annoyed eye roll, then looked back at Marshall. "So, you want to escape."

"But not before our friends get here," Marshall said, and he put the woman down gently next to him.

The hallway door creaked open, and Marshall was stunned at the sight of Elizabeth.

"Lizzie?" Marshall shouted with joy.

Athena and Alan glanced at each other with confused looks. Marshall gave Elizabeth a huge bear hug, while Castor welded the maintenance door shut. The guards would have to circle around the other side of the ringed hall to get back to them. The teleporter tried to run, and Alan - while still making eye contact with Athena - held out a hand to hold her in place with his mind.

"What's going on here?" Athena asked.

Marshall looked at Alan and Athena, a huge grin on his face. "This is Lizzie. She's my sister."

sixteen

"We have to get out of here," Elizabeth said. "They're coming for us. He's almost here."

"Okay, okay, you'll go through with the teleporter and make sure she keeps the portal open long enough for us all to make it through," Marshall explained, his eyes on the woman standing idle next to Castor.

"I have a name, you know," the woman replied rudely.

"I bet you do," Castor said, arms folded and voice annoyed. He looked at her uniform, "Song? What kind of name is *Song*?"

"It was my mother's," Song answered.

"She shoulda' kept it," Castor replied jokingly.

"Shut up," Marshall snapped, "Let's go, *now.*"

Athena looked at Song.

"Whatever her name is, she's going to betray us," Athena said nonchalantly. The woman's eyes bulged, bewilderment stricken on her face. Athena looked in the woman's eyes with a searching, piercing expression. "She's going to drop us in… a quarry."

The woman cleared her throat.

"That's a lie. I wouldn't…"

"We can read minds, you idiot," Elizabeth chimed in. "Lying isn't going to get you anywhere. But if you cooperate, you'll be fine."

"Do you know what they'll do to me if I help you?"

"Do you know what I'll do?" Elizabeth replied sharply. The woman flinched as she felt bugs crawling on her skin. She looked down and saw hundreds of spiders climbing up her arms, winding their way to her face. Hundreds of tiny, bristled legs tapping away at her goosebumped skin. Song screamed.

"Oh god, get it off. Get them off!" Song shrieked.

"Lizzie, cut it out," Marshall complained.

Elizabeth stopped, and Song was fine again, save for the hyperventilating. Marshall put a hand on Elizabeth's shoulder.

"We don't have time for this," Elizabeth said coldly to Marshall. "He'll be here any moment."

"Who?" Castor asked.

"The *Director*," Athena said. "He's back from DC, and if I'm reading this right, he's totally pissed."

The doors to the hub creaked where Castor had welded them shut. Alan looked back at Marshall, who seemed to be growing more concerned by the minute. Marshall turned to Song.

"Open a portal. Somewhere remote."

Song hesitantly nodded, flicked her wrist, and opened a blue portal next to the group. Elizabeth looked at Marshall, her eyes frantic.

"I'll be right behind you. I promise."

Elizabeth went through the portal with the operator. Castor nodded to Athena for their turn.

"You did good, kid," Castor said to Alan. "Sorry for giving you so much shit."

Alan nodded, but his eyes were on Athena. Ever since that first day they met in the lobby, Alan's eyes had been on her. Now there were silent words passing between them. A message Alan couldn't forget. He'd never forget that moment bathed in red light in the closet. It seemed to be the only moment worth remembering now. But they didn't say a word. They just stared at each other, as

Athena walked backward into the portal, and vanished. Castor walked in after her.

"We're running out of time, the portal's starting to weaken," Marshall said, as he looked at the hub door beginning to split under the pressure of the Department's full force.

"Go. I'll hold them back," Alan said softly.

"You can't," Marshall shouted. "That's an entire army through those doors."

"You have a family that needs you, Marshall. You need to go. Now."

"I won't," Marshall refused.

"You don't have a choice."

The doors split enough for a guard to stick his handgun through and fire a shot. Alan held his arm out and stopped the bullet in mid-air.

"Don't worry about me. This is what I want."

Alan turned his other arm and pushed Marshall with his mind, watching him dissolve into the portal as it disappeared.

~ ~ ~

Marshall fell backward into a misty forest. The others were standing around the operator, who was passed out on the ground. He watched the portal slowly dissolved as he sat up. Marshall looked at his friends with panic.

"No, no. No, I have to go back. Open another portal," Marshall begged.

Elizabeth looked down at Song, who was lying on the grass, her eyes closed and sweat covering her glossy face.

"It took too much out of her, Marshall. We can't."

Marshall stood up and punched the nearest tree he could see as hard as he could. The tree splintered like a twig, sending shards and chunks of wood into the air and into other trees, knocking them down as well.

~ ~ ~

A lot of bullets. Alan could feel his brain boiling as he tried to stop them all. He pushed back on the guards with all he had in his tank. They flew through the air like dolls. Then the operators came. At first, he could defend himself. The punches and other telekinetics were easier to block than a hail of bullets. But

172

eventually his mind couldn't handle the workload. There were too many, and their blows pierced through his defenses.

Punched to the floor. Alan coughed blood. He strained to see through his swollen eye. The operators had parted.

The Director had arrived.

The gray-haired man, in his navy suit, with his perfect smile, and his piercing eyes stood before the kid with the smart mouth, the failing brain; the instigator of an insurrection.

"Mr. Mitchell," the Director said, his voice loud and authoritative.

"You know, eventually I'm going to get your friends. Every last one of your little band of freaks. Anyone who planned this little cabal is going to get what they deserve."

Alan could feel his knees bleeding as they scraped on the metal grate floor, his eyes peering up into the fluorescent light of the teleportation room. Luckily, the Director didn't know their faces, so he wasn't sure who he was dealing with; save for Alan and probably Athena.

"Such excruciating pain awaits the terrorists who think they can oppose us," the Director said with disdain, and he nodded to the operator looming over Alan. The operator pushed his hand into

Alan's shoulder, releasing a jolt of pain inside Alan's brain. Alan groaned in agony and lifted his head up as best he could.

"It was me. It was all me. I roped them into it. Everyone else wanted to keep working. It's all my fault; all of it," Alan said through clenched teeth, tears of pain streaking down his face, mixing with the blood and sweat into a stinging concoction.

The operator standing over him pressed further into Alan's brain, tormenting Alan with images of his friends dying. It was all fuzzy chaos, but Alan could feel the raw emotion of loss and tragedy, even though the faces were blurry.

The Director kept a straight face, his emotions under control. He looked at the operator, and then back down at Alan. Little more than twenty years, the Director guessed, but he was trouble regardless.

"Good. I don't want to waste any more time. We're going to clean this up in one strike. Do you know what I'm going to do, Mr. Mitchell?"

The Director bent down, staring at Alan's wincing visage. Alan looked at the Director's cold, icy-blue eyes, and knew it would be truly horrific.

"No," Alan groaned through his teeth, "But I have a feeling it's not going to be pleasant."

The Director let a rumbling laugh slip through his diaphragm. His eyes peered into Alan's wavering gaze. The operator pressed his hand further into Alan's shoulder, and Alan yelped like a kicked dog.

"I'm going to make it so you were never born, Mr. Mitchell. Not a soul will know you ever existed on this mud ball. Your parents won't even have an inkling of your soul," the Director's quick-worded tirade was laced with venomous hate. He paced as he spoke, as if his hatred gave him energy to carry on.

"How is that-," Alan winced as he started to lose feeling in his lower legs, "How is that possible?"

The Director looked down at Alan with pity. The boy had clearly gone through hell to save his friends, but he had grown from an inconvenience to a threat; and the Director could not abide threats. The Director placed a gloved hand on the top of Alan's head.

"When time is on your side, anything is within your grasp, Mr. Mitchell. Anything," the Director was waxing poetic, the situation truly within his control.

"Time?"

"I'm going to go back and keep you from being born, and we'll be able to put this whole thing behind us. Maybe I won't have to kill your friends, or maybe I will just for the hell of it. Who knows?" the Director enjoyed his threats. They gave him power. Even now, as he began thinking about the past, he could feel the world swelling around him. It was a great symphony of light and warmth. He put a hand on Alan's head.

"Goodbye, Mr. Mitchell; I'm afraid, for the last time," the Director walked backwards as a bubble - its contents a mirror of the world around them - grew out of thin air. Alan looked at the Director and realized - in seeing his devilish smirk - that he wouldn't stop at just killing Alan. No, this would continue until his blood lust was sated. Alan felt a thumping in his chest, his heart beating with a ferocity he'd never known before.

Alan desperately pushed the operators off of him with his mind. He tried to reach the Director, who entered the bubble, then a massive shockwave struck Alan. Everything went black.

~ ~ ~

The diner was empty this early in the morning. One waitress was attending to a hitchhiker and his coffee refills, but that was all the customers up front. Marshall sat with his group in booths lining the outer wall of the diner, chewing on eggs and bacon.

"I missed bacon so much," Castor said, his voice humming with a near lust-level of pleasure. Athena rolled her eyes and took a sip of hot, black coffee.

The TV overhead was blaring the local news when a breaking bulletin appeared, cutting the regular news short. It was a special announcement from Director Robert Orson of the Department for Mutated Persons, the same Director who had tortured them for years.

He stepped to his podium and began speaking.

"This morning, the Department was viciously attacked by genetic terrorists seeking to harm our way of life. Their leader, Alan Mitchell, killed and wounded hundreds of honest Americans who were working to keep our people safe. We cannot abide acts of terrorism. We cannot continue to allow genetic deviations to cause destruction and terror on our watch.

"We have brought Alan Mitchell to justice, but we are not safe from future attacks. But this event has given our government reason for a meaningful response. I have received a mandate from our government to expedite the search for genetically abnormal people living within our borders. We will keep this country safe. We will not flinch in the face of terror. Thank you."

"What a load of bullshit," Castor grumbled, his fork stirring his scrambled eggs clockwise into his plate.

"Do you think Alan is really dead?" Athena asked.

Marshall looked up at Athena, her eyes pleading for the lie she wanted to hear; the lie Marshall couldn't dare to tell her. He looked at his sister Elizabeth, who was keeping guard over the passed-out operator, Song.

Marshall remembered the exact moment Alan changed his mind. Right before Alan jumped out of Marshall's bathroom window to escape.

"Some people think they can escape hell by living in it right now," Alan replied. "Your family will never be safe, no matter how much you punish yourself to protect them. Eventually we'll all be rounded up like cattle, and your sacrifice won't mean a damn thing to the people suffering then. I know I was cynical. I was wrong. You can make a difference. You have to at least try. Otherwise, none of this means anything. We can't wait for them to change their minds or for things to fix themselves because they won't. We have to fight."

Marshall looked at Athena, the tears visibly welling up in her eyes.

"We have to free more of our friends. We have to find my family. I have four more brothers and sisters, and they'll help us against the Department. We have to unite the six. Alan wanted us to fight."

"Then that's what we'll do," Athena replied, steeling herself against sadness. She turned it into righteous anger. The others nodded. "For Alan."

~ ~ ~

The girl - no more than seven, with dark hair and tan skin - played in the meadow, a beautiful open field with a large tree in its midst. She split the tall grass, frolicking into a perfectly manicured lawn sitting in the shadow of the tree. She tossed her periwinkle dress to the left and right as she skipped to the tree, a wonderful apple tree. The girl stopped abruptly as she saw the figure of a man face down next to the tree. She picked up a loose branch from the foot of the tree and poked the body out of curiosity.

"Hello?" she called out. "Hello? Are you okay?"

The man groggily pushed himself up and turned his body to look at the little girl.

"I'm," the man looked up at the girl. "I'm fine."

"Are you, Mr. Mitchell?" the girl asked, her tone more concerned than before.

Alan gave her a curious look, raising his arm to block the light from his eyes, and saw his watch - the watch Molly gave him - ticking away as if it had never broken.

"Where am I?" Alan asked, as he felt his body still in agony from the beating he took. The girl smiled and held her hand out to Alan.

"Welcome to the in between."

To be continued in

HUNTED BETWEEN WORLDS

about the author

Robert R. Fike is an author and designer from San Antonio, Texas. You can find him on twitter (@robfike) if you'd like to talk writing, art, and the Department for Mutated Persons.

Robert hopes that this book found you exactly when you needed it, and that you will continue to see the wonder in others and in yourself. He can't wait to share the next installment in the Department for Mutated Persons, and that you would share your love for the story with your friends, family, complete strangers, aliens (if/when they show up), and anyone else you happen to bump into.

Don't forget to check out all the exciting stuff that's going to come by following Robert on twitter (@robfike) and bookmarking his website (www.robfike.com). Also, don't forget to review this book as it helps more people discover it.

You are mighty.

Made in the USA
Lexington, KY
24 August 2019